Moon D🐕G

JANE ELSON

HODDER CHILDREN'S BOOKS

First published in Great Britain in 2020 by Hodder and Stoughton

1 3 5 7 9 10 8 6 4 2

A CIP catalogue record for this book
is available from the British Library.

ISBN 978 1 444 95570 5

Typeset in Egyptian 505 and DIN Light by Avon DataSet Ltd, Bidford-on-Avon, Warwickshire

Printed and bound in Great Britain by Clays Ltd, Elcograf S.p.A.

The paper and board used in this book are made from wood from responsible sources.

MIX
Paper from
responsible sources
FSC® C104740
FSC
www.fsc.org

Hodder Children's Books
An imprint of Hachette Children's Group
Part of Hodder and Stoughton
Carmelite House
50 Victoria Embankment
London EC4Y 0DZ

An Hachette UK Company
www.hachette.co.uk

www.hachettechildrens.co.uk

For Nahum, Benjamin and Timothy

Dedicated to the memory of Crayon –
a brave little kitten who fought so hard
and changed my life, leading me on
to the path of rescue animals.

#AdoptDontShop #LucysLaw

1

Marcus

The day I, Marcus Sparrow, first met Moon Dog was no ordinary day. It started with me doing what any kid with half a brain would do if they were about to be shouted at.

GET AS FAR AWAY AS POSSIBLE!

So here I am in PJs at the bottom of our garden, sitting on top of a pile of old fruit-and-veg crates from Nana Sparrow's market stall. This is my favourite thinking place. The crates are piled up in the corner against the fence which divides our house from the empty house next door. There's a hole in the fence, just big enough for me to poke my hand through and waggle it around. I like to do this when I'm thinking my thoughts.

As my hand is officially trespassing into next

door's garden, waggling round and round, it's like the air between me and our back door is on fire, crackling, just waiting for my nana's shouting to zap through it.

I hear a bellow from somewhere inside our house.

'MARCUS!'

The back door crashes open and Nana Sparrow comes marching into the garden. Her jaw juts out, her mouth is screwed up and her long grey hair is scraped up in a tight bun on the top of her head. She is holding broken bits of a figurine in one hand but before she reaches me, something wet and cold with what feels like warm, velvety fur around it, rests itself in my trespassing palm. I fall off my crates in shock and look down at my hand. Gungy drool drips from it. I wipe it on the grass and scramble back up, climbing to the top of the crates to look over the fence.

A giant black bear of a dog gallops up the grass and disappears through the back door. It was his nose I felt, resting in my hand. He obviously wants to make friends with me. I'm

2

sure it's a Newfoundland. In the *Encyclopaedia of Dogs A-Z* it lists them as one the world's largest dogs.

The empty house next door is for sale. Maybe he belongs to people who are looking round it? Oh, I want them to buy it and then I would be next-door neighbours with an actual Newfoundland dog and I can offer to take him for walks and play with him and . . . I shut my eyes, cross my fingers and make a wish.

Nana's hand grabs my arm.

'MARCUS, LOOK AT ME WHEN I'M SHOUTING AT YOU.'

My dog dreams had blotted out Nana Sparrow's shouting, and the fact that I'm about to be in BIG TROUBLE!

I jump off the crates and spin round so I'm facing her – well, to be truthful I'm looking down on her 'cause I'm taller than Nana.

'How, Marcus? How did you manage to break it?'

'I am Marcus Sparrow, with hands as big as dinner plates, and the kind of feet that other

3

kids trip over,' I say. 'That's why the stupid ornament broke.'

Nana Sparrow opens up her hand and looks down at the broken figurine. It's a lady in a bonnet, carrying a basket of fruit. Only, the china lady in a bonnet doesn't have a basket of fruit any more and, come to think of it, she doesn't have a head either.

'It's not my fault, is it,' I say, 'that my feet cause vibrations when I'm walking about. The house builders should make stronger floors that don't go vibrating all over the place, making ornaments fall and smash.'

I see Nana's lip twitch, like she's about to laugh, but then she looks me up and down.

'AND WHY ARE YOU IN THE GARDEN IN YOUR PYJAMAS? WHAT WILL THE NEIGHBOURS THINK?'

I am about to tell her about the Newfoundland dog that might become our neighbour, but something stops me. I don't want to say it out loud 'cause I might jinx it, and the longing to have a dog in my life is like a belly ache that

4

never ever goes away. I decide then and there to keep it secret.

So I say, 'But Nana Sparrow, we've got no neighbours next door to see me in my pyjamas and none the other side 'cause we're the end house in the street, remember?'

'Oh, you!' she says and snorts with laughter. And then she starts chasing me round the garden, and we are running round and round, laughing our heads off, but she can't catch me, 'cause I'm too fast for her. Then she stumbles and drops the bits of the figurine china lady, so I go back to help her and she suddenly looks so sad.

'I bought that for your mum and dad's wedding present,' says Nana.

I swallow hard and take a big breath before saying in my bestest, most gentle voice, 'Mum's not lived here since I was seven, and she's never coming back, so she's not going to care. And Dad won't even notice 'cause he's spent the last four months and three days in bed under his sadness cloud.'

Just then I look up and see my dad is standing in the back doorway, in his pyjamas, staring at us with a face full of emptiness. But I don't want Dad's face to be empty, I want it to be full of thoughts. So I grab the broken bits of the china lady out of Nana's hand and run towards him.

'Look, Dad,' I shout, 'I've broken it. The china lady's got no head, I've smashed your wedding present.' And I wait to be told off. I wait for him to shout at me . . . but there is nothing.

It's like I haven't even said any words.

He turns round and walks out of the kitchen and I hear him go up the stairs and his bedroom door swing shut and the creak of his bedsprings as he gets back into his broken three-legged bed with a fourth leg made out of a pile of books.

My anger starts to fill me up. Red-hot anger, bubbling through me. And before I know it I am stomping upstairs and as my feet jar into each wooden step it feels good. I slam my bedroom door and the whole house shakes.

I kick through the heaps of clothes on the floor, stare in the mirror at my sticking-up black hair and chocolate-brown eyes (with not-slept-for-months shadows under them) and fling myself face down on my bed. The mattress creaks.

I hear Miss Raquel's voice in my head. *Come on, Marcus – breathe out anger and breathe in love. Come on, Marcus, you can do it.*

I try, but I don't think I know what love looks like right now. I imagine my anger pouring out of me and filling my bedroom, my house, my street, the world, and gradually I feel calmer. But then sadness fills my anger-emptied body.

I swing my legs round so that I am sitting on the edge of the bed. I hear Dad's snoring from his room.

Nana pokes her nose round my door. 'Marcus, school now! Shift yourself. Come on, it's Friday. One more day to get through, then you've got your weekend to laze about.'

Her words are cross but there are stars of kindness in her eyes. I look at my small, strong

Nana Sparrow, with her legs and hands gnarly and knobbly as tree branches, and a catapult of guilt pings me in my gut.

'Sorry, Nana, didn't mean to break your old china lady.'

She sniffs. 'I dare say you didn't. You're just big boned.'

I take a breath and try for the hundred millionth time. 'I wouldn't break so many things if I had a dog. I would be out from under your feet, walking my dog on the heath, not indoors breaking china ladies' heads off. Please, Nana Sparrow. I want a dog. I need a dog; a dog would be a friend.' I don't say: a dog wouldn't leave me like Mum did. But I'm thinking it. 'Please, Nana Sparrow. Pleeeeease.'

An extra big snore comes from next door.

Nana sighs. 'I can't even cope with your dad, never mind a dog messing up the place with muddy footprints. And while we're at it, you've got till tomorrow evening to pick all those dirty clothes off the floor and put them in the laundry basket. Get yourself dressed and off to school,' she says. 'Now.'

And I know this dog argument is lost but I'm not giving up. Not ever.

As I've already told you, my house is right at the end of Mabel Street. I look up at next door's window, hoping to catch a glimpse of the dog, but I think the people looking round must have gone. The Grayson & Stoat estate agents' FOR SALE sign has come loose and is tipping over, into the street. It's always doing that – like someone keeps messing with it. I open the squeaking gate, step into next door's front garden and heave the FOR SALE sign back up again so that it's not lying in the middle of the pavement for a blind person to trip over, or for a dog to bump into and hurt themselves. Mr Anderson used to live next door, but he's gone to work in Hong Kong and his house seems to have been empty for ever.

I feel a pair of eyes on me from the upstairs window of the empty house, but when I look up, no one is there.

I hurry up my street and see Matt the Vet ahead of me getting into his VET ON CALL car. I wave and he smiles and waves back. Matt came to our school to talk about the rescue dogs from the Beckham Animal Rescue Centre. I asked so many questions that he ended up staying an extra hour. He said that he would never forget me.

I continue towards Grayson & Stoat estate agents on the corner. I am just thinking what a rubbish estate agents they are 'cause Mr Anderson's house has been empty for ages, when a boy wearing the same Heath Academy navy blue school-uniform-of-dread steps out of the doorway and straight into me.

IT'S NICO FROM YEAR 9. OH, NO, NO, NO! He eats Year 7s like me for breakfast. I'm sure of it.

'Sorry,' I say, even though it was *him* that bumped into me.

'You better be,' he says, and turns on his heel and struts off.

I duck behind a tree and wait, 'cause obviously

I don't want to walk to school with the Year 7-muncher . . .

While I wait, I look behind me at the hill on the heath and imagine walking my very own dog there, but my stomach flips as I see the tangled ruins of Rose Manor Hall looming at the very top of the hill. It burned down back in olden Victorian times and is meant to be haunted.

I count to one hundred then leave the safety of my tree and turn into Cinder Street. Walking towards me, through the swarm of kids all making their way towards Heath Academy's school gate, is my favourite Staffie, Flora, with her owner Alf, who cleans my nana's windows. He's as small and stocky as Flora herself.

'Hello, girl,' I say, kneeling on the pavement as Flora runs up to give me a Staffie kiss. I fling my arms around her brown coat.

Even though it's only just around the corner, it always takes me the longest time to get to school, even on the best of days, because I've gotta say hello to any dog I pass on the way.

11

'All right, Marcus.' Alf nods. 'Flora loves her friend Marcus, don't you, girl?'

'I could give Flora a walk for you Alf, save your legs.'

Alf grins at me. 'Nice try, Marcus. Nana Sparrow would have my legs for firewood if she thought I'd delayed your book learning. Now get yourself to school.'

I grin back and run through the school gate, but the stupid strap on my bag snaps. As my bag hits the ground, red bubbling anger cuts through me, and I give my bag an almighty kick. A group of Year 7s back away.

'All right, boys,' I say, waving and turning on a smile. 'Do you fancy a quick game of footie before the bell goes?' I call after them as they head towards the school doors.

But they don't turn round. I hate that just 'cause I'm the biggest boy in Year 7 – actually, I'm the biggest boy in the lower school – the other kids are scared of me. I still haven't made any friends since I started Heath Academy.

There's a slow clapping. I turn round. It's Nico.

'Nice kick, Marcus. Getting vexed over a bag? I like it. What, you thought I never saw you, hiding behind that tree?' he says, grabbing my ear.

'Sorry,' I say. 'I never meant to knock into you. Really sorry, sorry, Nico . . .'

He gives me a killer stare, then slowly smiles through gritted teeth.

'Marcus, my man, no sweat. Sol wants a word with you, as it goes.'

A group of giggling, whispering Year 8 girls walks past us.

'Wait there,' hisses Nico to me before he struts up to them.

'Remember what I said, girls – no going up to Rose Manor Hall, or the ghost children will get you.'

The girls run away, squealing.

He chuckles before turning to me and saying, 'This way.'

My heart thuds in time with my footsteps as we walk over to where Sol is leaning, still and deadly, against the wall by the bins. He is the leader of the Cinder Street Boyz. He is dead hard; his brother is in Young Offenders. In our school, if Sol wants words with you, you don't say no. Baz, the fool of the Cinder Street Boyz, is hopping from foot to foot.

Sol looks me up and down.

'Marcus, we was wondering if you wanted to hang out with us? We could do with someone of your . . . stature, shall we say?'

'Yeah, you'll have your uses,' says Nico.

'What, me? In the Cinder Street Boyz . . . ?'

'You'll have to do an initiation,' says Baz.

If I'm in the Cinder Street Boyz, I'll belong. I'll have friends and no one will mess with me. I'll be able to do what I want and . . . and Nana Sparrow will kill me.

I bump fists with Nico, Baz and Sol. The school bell goes, and I try and copy their lolloping, hard-boy walk, but I don't think I've quite got it right. Then a little hand pushes me aside and I stagger off balance, as the tiniest girl, with long black spirally hair, storms through the middle of the Cinder Street Boyz.

They all start laughing.

She spins round, fury in her big brown eyes. She flicks her hair behind her ears.

'What's so funny? I am trying to get to school and you lot are blocking my way.'

'Junior school's in Kentish Town, little girl. Heath Academy's for big people,' says Baz and the Cinder Street Boyz slap hands and crack up laughing.

'Yeah, little girl, the fairy what me mum puts on top of our Christmas tree is bigger than you,' says Sol.

'You are so tiny—' bursts out of my mouth before I can stop myself and I hate myself for it when I see the look in her eyes.

'Yeah, well, my fist might fit into a teacup but if any of you lot ever try to hang me on top of a Christmas tree, you're finished! Do you hear me? So don't even try it.'

'Has anyone ever told you that you are cute?' Nico smirks.

'AND I HATE IT WHEN PEOPLE TELL ME I'M CUTE!'

She spins round and runs off.

A sparkler explodes in my heart.

'See ya later,' I mumble to the Cinder Street Boyz, and tear after her.

''Scuse me . . . Stop, please.'

The tiny girl turns round.

'Are you new?'

She nods.

'In Year 7?'

'Yeah,' she says.

'I'm Marcus. Marcus Sparrow.'

'I'm Delilah Jones,' she says.

'I'll take you to the school office, Delilah Jones,' I say.

Her mouth blossoms into a full-blown smile that illuminates her whole face, and my eyes just feel like they're stuck to her with a magnetic force. Delilah is tremendous. She's got sad eyes though. I think my sadness has reached out to hers and bumped fists.

I wonder if she would be friends with me?

2

Delilah

I wonder if he would be friends with me?

Marcus smiles back. He was with those horrendous boys though, so maybe not. But come to think about it, he didn't laugh at their worthless mocks about my size, so I don't think he's like them. His eyes are kind. It doesn't look as if he's slept much. I think us people who don't sleep much recognise that in each other, like a secret club.

'The school office is this way,' says Marcus, marching back down the corridor. Kids jump to get out of his way as he bulldozers through them.

'Don't worry, I'll look after you,' he says, looking back over his shoulder.

'STOP RIGHT THERE,' I say. 'I don't need looking after. I can look after myself, thank you very much.'

Marcus looks hurt and confused, like I've punched him in the belly.

I feel mean.

'Do you know where the school office is?' he asks.

'No,' I say. 'But . . .'

'Well then,' he says, and carries on bulldozing down the corridor.

'Marcus,' I shout, as I get pushed this way and that. 'Wait, MARCUS!' Rucksacks bang into me from all sides, nearly having my eye out, which is one of the distinct disadvantages of being the smallest person in the school. I hear giggles and whispers and even a couple of, 'Ahhh, look how cute she is.'

Marcus ploughs back through the swarm of kids, reaches down, grabs my arm and pulls me after him.

Not that I need rescuing. I two million per cent don't, it's just 'cause I am knee-high to a grasshopper, as my dad used to say.

Dad.

It's happened again. I have these moments, these breaths of a second, where I forget he has gone.

I stop in my tracks and bite my lip hard and blink

18

my eyes quickly, but Marcus is looking down at me. He saw, I think.

My phone buzzes. I search for the red case in my bag.

Have you arrived at school?

Another text from Mum. To go with all the other texts she has sent me this morning.

Have you reached the bus stop?

Are you on the bus?

Have you got your purse?

Have you got your pencil case?

I text back:

At school buzy can't talk

And then add **xxx** so she knows I love her. I just wish she would stop checking up on me all the time.

I drop the phone back into my bag and run to catch up with Marcus.

We walk past a closed door that says *Mr Lawson, Head Teacher* on a brass plaque.

Marcus stops at the door next to it and knocks. 'Come in,' shouts a voice from the other side.

A woman with long blonde hair tied in a ponytail is putting a plaster on this kid's bleeding finger.

'Hi, Miss,' says Marcus. 'I'm being helpful, like what you said to be. I've brought you the new girl.'

Then Marcus turns to me and says, 'Miss Raquel is who you go to if you get sick and also she gets bossed about by Mr Lawson, our head teacher.'

'I'm Mr Lawson's personal assistant, Marcus,' says Miss Raquel, laughing. 'It's my job to get bossed about. You must be Delilah,' she says to me. 'Welcome to Heath Academy. I've just had your mum on the phone, checking to see if you reached school.'

Before I can stop myself, I roll my eyes to the ceiling, which immediately makes me feel disloyal.

'Sorry,' I say, 'it's all right, Miss, I texted her.'

'Ah, we have a rule here, phones are handed over to us in the morning, and you collect them at the end of the day.'

As I undo my bag my special keyrings jangle against each other. I scrabble deep in the bag for my red phone, and shove it into her hand. 'Please, Miss, just take it,' I say, breathing a sigh of relief. I'll have freedom from my mum's worrying at school at least. I never thought in all my days I would be glad of a school rule.

'Miss Raquel's all right as it goes, for someone what works in a school,' says Marcus.

'High praise indeed,' says Miss Raquel, laughing. 'Marcus, phone?' she says, holding out her hand to him.

'No, Miss, I've still not got a new one. It's not fair! What is the point of a phone if you can't even sit on it without it smashing? Nana Sparrow's still vexed at me.'

Then Miss Raquel looks at me and smiles, and as she draws a breath to speak, I'm thinking, *Please, please don't say it. Please don't say: Marcus, will you look after Delilah?*

But she doesn't. She looks at us from one to the other and back again, and says, 'Look after each other.'

I like Miss Raquel. She hands me a pile of exercise books and textbooks, which I shove in my bag.

'Delilah is in Form 7T with you,' says Miss Raquel. 'You had better get to art.'

Marcus grins. 'Come on,' he says, 'this way.' And as I trot to keep up with him, as we go back down the corridor and climb a flight of stairs and along another corridor and up some more steps, I wonder, *Will I ever find my way around this school?*

Marcus pushes the door open into a big, sunny room. The other kids are already sitting on stools in front of their art easels, and my breath stops when I see how high the stools are. How am I going to get up there?

Everyone turns round and stares at me, and I want to just disappear and never come back. Panic starts to rise and rise and fill me up.

'What are you lot staring at?' says Marcus, and everyone quickly goes back to their conversations. It's as if they're a bit scared of him. I follow Marcus to the back of the class where two stools and easels are waiting. Marcus bends his knee and sticks his foot out above the ground.

'Step on it,' he whispers.

And I do, using his foot like a stepladder, and find myself on the stool, no trouble.

'I owe you one,' I whisper.

'It's all right,' he whispers back.

'No, I do,' I whisper. 'I always, always, pay my

debts. There will come a time when you'll need me.'

Then the teacher comes in, and I thank my lucky stars that everyone's attention is off me.

Marcus says, 'That's Mr Burnett. He's all right for a teacher.'

Mr Burnett is wearing a big white shirt, jeans and has a goatee beard. His eyes fall upon me, and I know it. I just know that he is about to do that awful thing that teachers do. That thing where they make the new kid stand in front of the whole class and tell everyone about themselves. I've been the new kid often enough to know this, but I can't do it. I can't get off the stool in front of everyone. I'll get stuck. And then I see Marcus doing a tiny shake of his head. It took barely a second, but I saw it, and Mr Burnett is looking straight at him.

'Ah, you must be Delilah,' he says, walking up to my easel. 'It is so lovely to have you in the class. Now, usually I ask my new pupils what their dreams are. What they wish for most in the world. But I don't need to ask you this today, Delilah.' He turns back to the rest of the class. 'Because our goal today, class, is to draw your dreams.'

23

I don't need to even think for a second about what mine is, because I know with every breath in my body. I lose myself in every swirl and swish I draw with my pencil. I try and take a peep at Marcus's drawing, but he has his back angled so that I can't see it.

I escape from my world into my picture. The class is silent; there's not even a whisper as the clock ticks.

'Pencils down. It's time to share,' says Mr Burnett. 'Front row, hold your pictures up.' And he goes through the class, row by row.

There are drawings of computer games, and footballers scoring a goal, and nail salons, and holidays, and designer trainers and skateboards and headphones . . . Then he gets to us.

'Delilah, Marcus, what have you drawn?'

And we both say at exactly the same time, 'A dog, sir.'

We look at each other, and laugh and laugh, and I look at his picture of a giant dog. I think it's a Newfoundland, and he looks at my picture of a tiny puppy, and we give each other a high-five.

3

Marcus

I feel a ball of warmness in my belly – this must be what happy feels like, because I had forgotten, to be truthful.

Me and Delilah the Tremendous have both drawn dogs, and that is the perfect start of a friendship.

'Come on,' I say, 'have you got packed lunch?'

Delilah nods.

'Do you wanna come to my bench, where I eat my lunch? I don't like eating in the school canteen,' I say. 'All that noise and food smells what don't go with each other. Makes me feel sick, and then there was this incident where I dropped my dinner plate on Daniel Margate's head. He was pulling bits of spaghetti out of his red hair all afternoon, but it was an accident, honest, only of course nobody believed me, did they?'

Delilah laughs a proper belly laugh, and she doesn't look quite so sad, just for a moment.

The keyrings dangling from her bag jangle as she walks. The corner of the tiny silver St Paul's Cathedral keyring catches in my school jumper.

'Stand still.' Delilah starts to unhook the keyring. I put out my hand to touch the tiny Jamaican flag that is dangling next to it, glinting in the sun.

'My dad gave me that. He was born there. And Mum gave me the silver Tower of London, London Eye and this St Paul's Cathedral, 'cause she is a Londoner through and through. My dad said it was to remind me of the two glorious heritages I am from, and 'cause they met and fell in love in London and made me.'

'That is properly special,' I say.

'Yes,' she says, freeing the keyring. 'It is.'

My bench is on a patch of grass to the right of the school gate where there are a few sycamore trees. It has a gold metal plaque on it engraved with the words *A place for quiet thinking*. So it's where I go to do my school thinking. It will be good to think with Delilah. Less lonely.

I open my bag. There are about ten apples rolling around in there. Delilah laughs.

'Oh my goodness! Are you going to eat all of those?'

'It's my nana,' I say. 'She's got a fruit-and-veg stall in Camden Market, and she uses me like the leftover bin. Here, have one.'

And we sit in silence doing our thinking, like the bench tells us to do, with the sun on our cheeks, crunching apples, and the question I am dying to ask, even though Nana Sparrow would tell me I'm rude, just grows and grows till it pops out of my mouth.

'Why are you so small?'

Fury pinpricks her eyes.

'Why are you so tall?'

I've got no words to say to that, so we just sit, munching our apples.

When she's down to the core she says, 'I just didn't grow. OK?'

'Oh,' I say. 'Well, I didn't stop growing.'

And we start laughing like it's the funniest thing in the whole world.

'Where do you live?' I ask.

'Twenty-three Beckham Estate, do you know it?'

'Everyone round here knows the Beckham Estate.' I grin. The Beckham Animal Rescue Centre is on the wasteland next to the estate. It's where Matt the Vet works.

'We're on the fourth floor,' she says. 'Only, it's one big mess. We just moved and DIY is not Mum's strong point and she won't let me have a go at carpentry and fixing things. Our house is not a home, as the saying goes. My mum worries a lot,' she says.

I notice she don't mention her dad; she must just have her mum looking after her, like I've got my nana.

'My dad sleeps a lot,' I say. 'He's got sadness. He used to be a handyman, putting up shelves

28

and stuff for people.' And the prickle of a plan starts to grow in my mind.

'Mum drives me nuts – she treats me like a little kid.' Delilah rolls her eyes. 'Just 'cause I'm small . . .'

And whatever else she was going to say just hangs in the air, hidden words.

'Well . . .' I pluck up every atom of courage I have and say, 'Delilah Jones, I think you are tremendous.' I feel my cheeks burning red.

She looks sideways at me, through her long eyelashes. 'So are you,' she says.

'We are both TREMENDOUS,' I say, and we high-five again, only this time it's a slow high-five, 'cause I think maybe I was a bit rough when I high-fived her in the art room, and I don't want to snap her hand off. So I hold my hand up and spread my fingers, and her tiny hand fits into the palm of mine and stays there.

I feel eyes on me, so I quickly drop my hand. I look up to see Sol, Baz and Nico in their favourite place by the bins, glowering over at us. I remember the gang initiation and my bones shiver.

What have I got myself into with them? Just 'cause I wanted some friends. But to be honest, I didn't have much of a choice. You don't say no to Sol.

'Those boys are rude,' says Delilah. 'I don't like them one little bit. I thought you was one of their gang when I saw you this morning.'

'No,' I say. 'I ain't part of any gang.' Which is technically not a lie 'cause I haven't done my initiation yet.

'I'm telling you, Marcus, stay away from them, 'cause they are bad news and if you ever start hanging out with them I will de-friend you.'

And I wish so much this morning had never happened, me banging into Nico, 'cause I don't want to be in the Cinder Street Boyz any more. I don't need them. I've got Delilah now.

I ignore the hard-boy looks they are shooting at me.

'Delilah,' I say. 'I'll tell you something, though you gotta promise not to laugh. Even though I've not got a dog, I've bought a feeding bowl and dog lead, all ready for when I do have one. I keep them under my bed, and I've even bought some dog toys and treats and stuff.'

Delilah bursts out laughing. 'Me too!' she says. 'I keep a dog lead hidden at the back of my wardrobe and I've even got a dog bed hidden there as well. Sky blue, it is. I've got everything ready for when Mum eventually says yes.'

We talk about our doggy dreams, but I decide not to tell Delilah about the Newfoundland in next door's garden. I'm keeping him my secret for now.

And then the most magical thing happens. Just as we are talking about dogs, a blue Staffie walks through the school gate. It is wearing a coat that says *Wilbur the Reading-Support Dog*. A woman with red hair is leading it towards the main building.

'Oh my days,' I say. 'I have seen those dogs on TV. They are to help kids who don't like reading. They read out loud to dogs, as dogs won't judge 'em. I never thought we would get one at Heath Academy. Come on, this way.' I jump up. 'If there's a dog in my school, I need to be near it!'

We scoop up our bags and race past the noisy, smelly canteen to the library.

Mrs Johnson, the librarian, bars me from coming in, her arms stretched against the door frame. She towers above me and her headwrap makes her even taller.

I duck down, peeping under her arm.

A small group of Year 7s and 8s are sitting on beanbags, including Daniel Margate, who looks a bit scared when he looks up and sees me. In fact to be truthful they are all staring at me with fear.

'Hi,' I say, but it's like I haven't spoken. I'm just trying to be friendly. I spy a register on the desk that says *Silver Reading Group* and written underneath is *reluctant readers*. AND THEY'VE GOT CAKES. CAKES!

Wilbur is lying across the feet of the red-haired woman, who is drinking tea with Miss Raquel.

'Marcus Sparrow, you are not in this reading group, go about your business please.'

'Oh, but Miss, I've got that reluctant reading thing. I've got it bad. I need help with my reluctance.'

Mrs Johnson is biting her lip, like she is trying not to laugh.

'Marcus, what about the books you have borrowed and should have brought back four weeks ago – weren't they . . . *World of Dogs*, *Universe of Dogs* and *Encyclopaedia of Dogs A-Z*?' She screws her mouth up, like she always does when she is telling people off, but she has a twinkle in her eye.

'They are under my bed, Miss. I tried to read them, but I couldn't, 'cause of my reluctance.'

This is a cross-your-heart-hope-to-die lie because I've read them all four times, but I need to meet Wilbur the Staffie.

'Enough of your nonsense,' says Mrs Johnson and she turns to Delilah. 'You must be our new Year 7 pupil. I'm Mrs Johnson, the librarian. We will have to fix you up with a library card.'

But Delilah is ignoring her and staring at Wilbur, and Wilbur is whining softly and staring back.

Delilah slips under Mrs Johnson's arm and plonks herself on a red beanbag opposite Wilbur. He runs over to her and she flings her arms around him and hides her face, and her tiny shoulders start to shake. Delilah is crying.

There is a silence as realisation hits people.

'They always know,' says the lady with the red hair.

I know what she means, 'cause dogs have a natural understanding of how people are feeling. Wilbur knows Delilah is sad, and he has come to her to give comfort. But why is she crying? She was all right a minute ago.

Mrs Johnson takes the Year 7s and 8s to another part of the library so Delilah can be sad in private.

'Marcus,' says Miss Raquel, 'I will look after Delilah. Thank you for your kindness to her.' She wraps me a slice of chocolate cake in a serviette, and sends me on my way to boring double maths.

Like I can even think about numbers, when my new friend is crying.

I'm in the midst of one of my Mum dreams; it's the one where I am running up and down the aisles of a supermarket, searching for her, shouting her name, but a stack of giant baked-bean tins come crashing down on my head—

I wake with a jolt. Nana Sparrow's pork chop with apple sauce and stewed apple with custard sit heavy in my belly.

'Waste not, want not,' Nana Sparrow had said at dinner – it's her favourite saying.

'I've made a friend, Nana,' I said, as she put my pudding in front of me.

'I hope he's a nice lad,' she said.

'She's a girl,' I said, 'and she's sad.'

'Eat your apple and custard,' she said, 'or you'll be no use to anyone.'

So I did. I shoved in the biggest mouthful and then my plan came spluttering out.

'Nana Sparrow, my friend Delilah, she needs—'

'Don't talk with your mouth full.'

So I swallowed, choking, splattering apple on to the table. Nana thumped me on the back and fetched a cloth.

'Nana,' I said, cleaning up the mess, 'my friend Delilah needs DIY help putting up shelves and stuff. She's just moved into the Beckham Estate and Dad needs work so I was thinking . . .'

'Ask your dad,' she said. 'Go on, try.'

I knocked on his bedroom door. There was no reply.

I opened the door and walked up to the bed. Dad was scrunched up in a ball under the quilt. I couldn't even tell if he was asleep or awake.

'Dad . . . Dad, I need your help.'

Still nothing, so I bent over to shake his shoulder. 'Please, Dad, will you help me? My friend Delilah needs to make her house a home.'

Dad's head emerged and he opened his eyes and muttered a half-said word and it could have been a yes. It could've been a no. It could've been a maybe. It could've been anything.

36

'Dad, I just want you to help my new friend Delilah.'

'George, please, help your son.'

I turned round. Nana Sparrow was leaning with her head against the wall and her eyes were shut.

I didn't want Nana to get a sadness cloud too, so I gave her one of our special long hugs before giving up on Dad and going back to my bedroom. Now I'm lying in bed, trying to count all the apple dishes we've eaten this week to send myself back to sleep, like other people count sheep: apple fritters, apple crumble, apple pie, apple chutney, apple strudel, apple pizza (that was disgusting – an all-time low, even for Nana Sparrow's mad cooking). But it's no good. Sleep escapes me.

I feel under my bed for my secret dog lead and bowl, and I think about reading the *Encyclopaedia of Dogs A–Z*, but then my fingers clasp Mum's silk scarf. It still smells a tiny bit of her perfume, the scent of springtime. It's wrapped around her '*Dear Marcus, I love you but I am not a good mother. I need to be with Luke, who loves me, so I can find myself blah, blah, blah*' letter. They are the only things I've got left of her.

As my fingers stroke the silk, I feel as if I'm about to choke. I try not to think about why I wasn't good enough to make Mum stay, or why I am not good enough to get Dad out of bed and . . . *breathe out anger, breathe in love*, like Miss Raquel said.

But I am breathing all the anger in, and all the love is escaping, and . . . and I can't breathe.

I jump out of bed. My thoughts are choking me so I have to get out of here. I need to do some calm thinking.

I trample over the clothes on my bedroom floor, run down the stairs, undo the bolts on the back door, and run out into the back garden.

I tread on the wet grass with my bare feet and head towards the pile of old fruit-and-veg crates at the bottom of the garden by the small peephole in the fence. I plonk myself down on them. Shivering in my pyjamas, I look up at the moon. I stick my hand through the hole in the fence and waggle it round and round, which calms me down.

The empty house next door stands deserted, a threatening shadow against the night sky. It makes me shudder, so I look up at the moon again.

I jump as something wet and cold and furry rests in my hand.

It's the dog's nose!

I hear a snuffling and a whimper and leap up, thick gunky dog dribble dripping between my fingers. I wipe my hand on my pyjama trousers and step on to the bit of the bottom crate that's sticking out, I peep over the fence. The ginormous black Newfoundland dog stares up at me with big brown eyes, and I now know what love looks like.

But what's he doing here in the middle of the night?

There's movement from the house. I look up and see the kitchen window sliding open. I duck down behind the fence and peep through the hole. Why would anybody be looking round the house in the middle of the night? That house is meant to be empty!

The low growl of a man's voice comes through the night air. 'There you go, Dog.'

And a handful of what looks like dog biscuits are thrown out of the window.

The Newfoundland trots over and starts sniffing for the biscuits in the overgrown grass.

The window shuts.

I wait.

Nothing . . .

I pull myself up and climb back on to the crates. I dangle my arm over the fence, and slowly hold my hand out, so as not to startle the Newfoundland.

The dog ambles over and sniffs my outstretched hand.

'Hello, boy, haven't you got a name?' I whisper. 'That man just called you Dog.'

Just then the moon shines down on the giant dog, with all her brightness.

And by her silver light I place my hand on

the dog's forehead, and whisper, 'I name you Moon Dog. What are you doing out in the middle of the night, Moon Dog?'

The back door of the house crashes open. I duck down just in time.

'Don't bang the door, you'll wake the whole neighbourhood,' says the same growly man's voice.

A torch is switched on. I peep through the hole in the fence and watch as two men – one tall with a shaved head and a ring through his nose, and the other short with sticking up hair – come out into the garden. A torch beam lights up a tattoo of a leopard on the top of the smaller man's arm.

Moon Dog runs away from the men and disappears into a makeshift shelter at the bottom corner of their garden, directly opposite the hole in the fence I am peeping through. It's made of old planks of wood cobbled together. It has a flat roof and three walls but the front is open. The huge dog cowers in the corner on top of what looks like an old towel.

The two men creep along the lawn to the shed halfway down the garden and start bringing out furniture, carrying it back over the grass and in through the back door of the house. First a yellow sofa, then a lamp and an armchair. No words are spoken; the men obviously don't want to attract any attention to themselves.

My brain ticks. Why are they shifting furniture in the middle of the night? Why are these two men and a dog in a deserted house?

The small man with the leopard tattoo whispers, 'They're interested in a French—' then muttered words I couldn't hear. Then the word 'paperwork' travels to me on the night breeze.

Nose-Ring Man nods. 'I've got it ready.'

I hardly breathe until the men go back inside. I whisper, 'Moon Dog,' through the hole in the fence. He looks straight at me, wagging his tail.

Nose-Ring Man opens the back door, quietly this time, and slinks halfway to the bottom of the garden. '*In,*' he commands Moon Dog. The enormous dog gets up and gallops to the house, and in through the back door.

Now the garden is empty, and it's like no one was ever there.

As I clamber back into my bed, the light of the silver moon peeps through the gap in my curtains on to me and my still-banging heart. What are those men up to? Why were they moving furniture and talking about French paperwork in the middle of the night?

Moon Dog wants to be my friend, or he wouldn't have rested his nose in my hand when I stuck it through the hole in the fence.

With every breath in my body, I, Marcus Sparrow, long to be Moon Dog's friend. I've just got to see him again and work out what is going on next door.

As I fall asleep, thoughts of Moon Dog and Delilah spin round and round in my head. If only Moon Dog was mine.

4
Delilah

As I lie in my bed, the stars shine through my window twinkling with thoughts of Marcus, my new friend. He called me tremendous! I like that.

'Tremendous,' I whisper into the night.

I say it out loud, to banish all the spooky shadow shapes in my bedroom.

'Tremendous,' I say, to the heap of curtain material on the floor.

'Tremendous,' I say, to the pile of yet-to-be-put-up shelves.

'Tremendous,' I say, a little louder, to the towering shadow of my tepee book-den in the corner.

'I AM TREMENDOUS!' I shout at the wardrobe, the biggest shadow shape of all.

'Delilah, what's wrong?' calls Mum.

'Nothing, Mum, I was having a nightmare,' I lie.

I always wear my hair in two plaits to stop it tangling at night, but they are pulling on my head too tight, so I loosen them and try and get comfortable on my sky-blue silk pillow. I turn on to my side and snuggle into the blue rabbit that Dad bought me, and stare into the dark hole through my open wardrobe door.

I wish I was like those kids in *The Lion, the Witch and the Wardrobe* and could go through the back of the wardrobe to reach another land. I wish my dad lived in Narnia. I'd push my way through my clothes, step over the dog bed hidden at the back, and out I'd run into his arms. If I could just hug him one more time . . .

The moon shines on the pile of Dad's old vinyl records. It's all I've got left of him since that lorry came round the corner too fast, and took him away from me.

My dad.

I hum the first bit of the chorus of the Tom Jones song he always used to sing to me, '*Mmm mm mmm . . . Delilah*'.

Our song.

MY SONG.

I was called Delilah after Dad's great aunty in Jamaica, but the song fits perfectly because our family surname is Jones, just like Tom's.

'La la la . . . Delilah,' I sing softly, but my throat closes, and I can't breathe. Dad and I will never ever sing that song together again, and I can't bear it.

I try to think of something else. And Marcus pops into my head.

Marcus is kind, I think so very kind, and Dad always said to look for that quality before I let anyone close to my heart. I cringe as I remember crying in the library, clinging to Wilbur the reading dog, and Marcus seeing it all.

I am glad it's the weekend and I won't see him for two whole days. Hopefully my embarrassment will have faded by Monday.

The reluctant readers never got Wilbur to listen to their stories, because Wilbur wanted to be with me. He stayed by my side all afternoon, even when Miss Raquel took me into her office and gave me a glass of lemonade, made with fresh lemons, and we talked and talked through all my sadness, till it was all squeezed from my belly, like the squashed lemons that made my drink.

'Can't you sleep?' It's Mum, standing in my bedroom doorway fiddling with the strawberry blonde ponytail dangling over her shoulder.

'No,' I say.

'Budge over,' she says, jumping in bed beside me.

'Mum, your feet are cold!'

She grabs my hand and holds it tight in the dark. I can feel the rough ends of her chewed fingernails and her ruby rings digging into me. 'I was chatting to Rosemary,' she says, 'on the phone earlier. I really must go and see her. She asked if we'd settled in yet.'

Mum sits up in bed. I watch her, as she looks around at the heap of waiting-to-be-hung curtains on the floor, and the pile of wood that should be shelves. She starts twiddling with the silver bracelet that Dad gave her for her birthday, that she never takes off. She always does this when her anxieties are at their highest.

'We'll make this feel like our home,' she says.

47

'But DIY is not your strong point, Mum,' I say.

'I'll get it sorted, you wait and see,' she says.

Then we lie there, quiet as quiet can be, and I feel like there is this big gaping hole inside me that used to be filled with Dad love. I need something to fill it up. I need to fill it back up with love. I need a . . .

'Dog,' I say out loud. 'A dog would make things better.'

'Oh, not that again,' groans Mum.

Dad and I used to play this game we called 'Tell Me Ten Reasons Why'. When I reached my tenth birthday, Dad said that they were the best ten years of his life. He said if I wanted something, I had to give a reason for every year that he'd known me. I like to imagine that if he was still here he would have changed our game to 'Tell Me Eleven Reasons Why'.

I sit up in bed and lean over, switching my sky-blue lamp on.

'Eleven Reasons Why,' I say.

'Number one: giving a dog a home is a good thing to do.

'Two: dogs are kind. It's good to be kind.

'Three: it would be company for me.

48

'Four: it would be company for you, when I am at school.

'Five: dogs are therapeutic. It said so on the TV.

'Six: I need therapy.'

'Ah! That's cheating,' says Mum. 'Numbers five and six are the same.'

'OK,' I say, 'number six: the dog can stay with me, and be my constant friend when I keep having to change schools and flats and lose all my other friends because you can't settle in one place.'

'None of the other places felt quite right,' says Mum. 'Your dad wouldn't have been happy living in any of them. I felt it in my heart.'

'But Mum, Dad's not with us any more. We have to make a life without him. You can't keep running away from your sadness.'

'I'll make this our home,' she says. 'I vow to.'

Ignoring her made-too-many-times vow, I carry on with my list.

'Number seven: walking the dog would keep me fit and healthy.

'Eight: the doctor said you need to do exercise to stop you feeling so sad, and you could walk the dog, because you said it yourself, you hate going to the gym, so a dog would be absolutely perfect for you.

'Number nine: um . . . what can nine be? Oh yes. We both need to socialise more, meet more people, and having a dog is the bestest way ever to do that, because when you are in the park with a dog, other people with dogs come up and talk to you.

'Ten: we would not waste food, 'cause you are always moaning on about that.'

'Don't be rude, Delilah.'

'Sorry, I'm not meaning to be rude, Mum. I'm just telling the truth. The dog could eat our leftovers – as long as they were healthy for its tummy.

'And eleven . . . oh, eleven! Mum, I need a puppy to love. I need something to love so much, 'cause I miss Dad, more than all the raindrops in the sky, more than all the feathers on all the trillions of birds flying in the sky. Please, Mum, please, I beg you. I can't bear this. I just can't . . .'

Mum looks at me for the longest time.

'Delilah, I am not promising anything. I've got enough to worry about without worrying about a dog as well.'

But Mum's 'I'm not promising anything' is the closest I have ever got with her, 'cause her one 'not promising anything', is an almost promise, right?

'Let's look,' I say before that almost promise vanishes, and I lean over, nearly falling out of bed, reaching under for my sky-blue laptop.

Switching on my laptop, I google *puppies for sale*. Mum puts her arm around me.

And we are lost in a world of pugs, poodles, French bulldogs and cockapoos and Cavaliers, and the cutest most adorable dachshunds and I am in heaven.

5

Marcus

I dream I am swimming in the icy sea with Moon Dog, holding on to him as he pulls me through the waves. Then the sun comes out, and we are running on the beach, kicking sand, squashing sandcastles. Mum and Dad are watching, laughing, holding hands. I run towards them, Moon Dog at my heels, reaching, reaching for them. The sun's rays dazzle my eyes and when a cloud rolls over them, silencing their brightness as it floats away, Mum and Dad and Moon Dog vanish in the sea mist.

Moon Dog!

I bolt upright in bed.

I run to my bedroom window and look down at next door's garden. The shelter and garden are empty. Moon Dog has gone.

I lean right out of my bedroom window to get a better look at the whole garden. Moon Dog is definitely not there. Let's face it, he'd be hard to miss. His shelter looks ragged and lonely. I need to make it better for him.

Remembering it's Saturday – YES, YES, YES! – I grab a green jumper off the pile of clothes on my floor instead of the navy blue school-uniform-of-dread, pull it on over my pyjamas and squash my feet into the nearest pair of trainers. I reach under my bed and pull out a blue rubber dog-toy bone and a packet of dog treats, and run out of my bedroom and down the stairs, out of our back door and right to the bottom of the garden. I look up at next door's house to check if there's any signs of life. When I'm sure there's nothing, I throw the dog-toy bone and the packet of treats over the fence, so my hands are free to climb to the top of the pile of crates. With my heart beating against my tonsils, I scramble over the fence into next door's garden, scooping up the dog bone and treats. I do a crouched-down run to the shelter.

'Right, my Moon Dog,' I whisper, 'cause in my heart he is mine, 'let's make this dump of a shelter a bit more interesting for you.'

I set to work. First, I rub the toy bone in the earth, so if the men see Moon Dog with the bone, they will think it's an old toy that another dog has lost, not a brand new one, planted in the shelter for Moon Dog by the boy next door who loves him.

I put the bone in the corner so that Moon Dog has something to play with. Then I open the packet of dog treats with my teeth and scatter them in the other three corners. Pulling up handfuls of grass, I cover the treats, so that the men won't see them and Moon Dog can have fun scavenging for them.

Satisfied with my handiwork, I sit back on my heels and look up at Mr Anderson's house and then at my house. No sign of life in either of them, which is good 'cause Nana Sparrow will kill me if she sees me in next door's garden. This would be pretty hard to explain.

But why were Nose Ring and Leopard Tattoo moving furniture in the middle of the night? Something is going on and I need to find out what. I run up to the back door and push it. It's locked. There is definitely no one there or Moon Dog would have heard me and run to the door, most probably barking his head off.

Cupping my hand, I look through the window. I can see the key is still in the lock of the inside of the back door. It's an old wooden door and there is a small gap between the bottom of the door and the kitchen floor. An idea grips me. I ram the door hard with my knee. Nothing. Then again, and again. I hear a jangle. I peer through the window; the key has fallen on to the door mat. I drop to the floor and squeezing my fingers under the gap I pull the mat, inch by inch, through the tiny gap to my side of the door, holding my breath as the key pops through.

I've done it!

I grab the key and put it in the lock. My hands shake as I turn the key. The lock clicks. I turn the handle and step inside the house and into the kitchen.

The walls are lined with lots of white cupboards. I quickly open them all, but they are empty. No sign of the French paperwork that the men were whispering about last night. A thought punches me. 'French paperwork' . . . I hope that doesn't mean that they are going to live in France with Moon Dog. I can't lose him when we are just becoming friends. I can't. Maybe they are only going on holiday.

I notice the cupboard door under the sink is slightly open, as if something is stopping it from shutting properly. I pull the door open to reveal a big cardboard box. Inside are lots of cheap mobile phones. The sort with a pay-as-you-go SIM. There is also a packet of white stickers and some biros lying on top of the phones. Someone has started the job of scrawling names on the stickers and sticking them on the phones. I read Paul, George, Mick, Craig, Barry – names, names, names. This doesn't make sense. Why would there be a box full of mobile phones, stashed in the cupboard under the sink in a house that is supposed to be empty?

I open the kitchen door and creep down the hall and step into the front room. There are closed shutters in the windows, daylight slicing through the slats.

The yellow sofa I saw them bring out of the shed in the middle of the night is in the centre of the room. The floorboards are bare and there is a huge wooden chest by the window. I walk across the room to it. The chest reaches as high as my shoulders so I have to stand on my tiptoes to peep in.

Inside the chest is one of those tall lamps on a stand, and lots of cushions. There is also a huge purple velvet curtain, a stripy rug, mugs, a kettle and a coffee machine.

I hear a car stop outside in the street.

I freeze.

The front gate squeaks.

I leap away from the chest and run out of the room, down the hall, through the kitchen and out of the back door, closing it behind me.

I snatch the key out of the back-door lock and put it in my pocket, run over the grass, scramble over the fence on to my thinking crates and land in a heap in my garden.

Hiding the key under my top crate, I run in my back door and through my kitchen, into the hall and stop in my tracks.

Dad is sitting on the bottom step, dressed, clutching his tool bag on his knee.

'Good morning, son,' he says. 'You said your friend needed shelves.'

My dad has got out of his three-legged bed to help me.

6

Marcus

'Don't just stand there gawping,' shouts Nana Sparrow from the top of the stairs. 'Your dad has offered to help your friend. I want you dressed and in the van in ten minutes.'

I race up the stairs. Nana clutches my arm as I reach the top step.

'I'm coming too,' she whispers. 'I don't want your dad driving.'

In ten minutes I'm already showered and dressed. I reach under my bed for my dog lead, and shove it in my pocket. It may sound stupid, but I like to take it with me when I go to new places; you never know when you might find a stray dog that needs help, and to be truthful I just like the feel of it in my pocket 'cause it's

59

like I've got my very own dog.

I race back down the stairs to my nana, who is standing by our open front door holding one of her huge apple pies.

'Quick, Marcus,' she says, and I run out into the street to where our van is parked, and my dad is waiting.

My used-to-be-quick-thinking, cool-dressing dad still looks half asleep; his face is puffy and I can't help but notice how his big belly hangs over his tracksuit bottoms. He has stubble on his face and his hair is now long, greasy and straggly. Shame burns me, and I hate myself for it.

Before climbing into Nana's van, I look up at Mr Anderson's house for any sign of life. There is still nothing. The windows stare down at me, empty and desolate, and the FOR SALE sign is firmly in the ground. Moon Dog, Nose Ring and Leopard Tattoo have definitely gone for now. I cross my fingers, close my eyes and make a silent wish, *Please, please let me see Moon Dog again*.

'My friend lives on the Beckham Estate,' I

say, as we all climb into the front of the van and click on our seat belts.

What's Delilah going to think about me turning up on her doorstep with my whole family? But I can't think about that now; the main thing is my dad has actually got out of bed.

Nana turns the van into the main road. Dad has his tool bag open on his knee, and he is running his hands gently over his spanner and his hammer, smiling, greeting them like friends he has missed.

We stop at the traffic lights. Ahead of us, to the right, sitting on a wall outside some shops, are the Cinder Street Boyz, feet kicking against brick, shouting cusses at a woman walking past with a pushchair. The Cinder Street Boyz are looking hard, like nothing would scare them in the whole wide world.

I look down at my feet so they won't notice it's me, but Nana's van says *Sparrow's Fruit & Veg* on the side in big bold letters, so there's no way they won't see it.

Sol spots me and nudges Baz and Nico. I see

61

them pointing and laughing at my dad. I quickly look the other way.

'Friends of yours?' says Nana.

'No,' I say.

Nana turns into the Beckham Estate and parks the van. In the distance, on what everyone round here knows as 'the wasteland', I can see the Beckham Animal Rescue Centre. Long ago it was a youth club, but that got closed down. This is a good use for the old building. I would love to work there when I am grown up, like Matt the Vet. I think of all the dogs in the rescue centre and my feet just want to run right over the wasteland to play with them all, but that's dreamland and this is now.

I am about to land my whole family on Delilah's doorstep.

We take the lift up to the fourth floor.

I ring the doorbell of number twenty-three.

Footsteps . . .

The door swings open. A thin, worried-looking woman with a scruffy ginger-coloured bun looks me up and down.

'Yes, can I help you?'

'Are you Delilah's mum?'

She nods, then all my words come tumbling out of my mouth at once.

'I am Marcus. Delilah's friend from school. She told me you needed to make your house a home. This here is my dad George. He's good at shelves and stuff.'

'Just show me what you need doing,' says Dad. 'I'm here to help.'

'Oh but, but I couldn't . . .' says Delilah's mum. But then she sees Nana Sparrow and starts laughing. 'It's you, the lady from the fruit-and-veg stall who helped me pick up all my potatoes.'

And then Nana starts laughing too. 'What a small world! I thought your face rang a bell! Rolling everywhere, they were, when you dropped your bag. I've brought you one of me apple pies to welcome you to the neighbourhood.'

'How very kind. I am Florence. Do come in.'

But before I can get through the door, Delilah steps in my path.

She glares at me.

'What are you doing here, Marcus?'

'I just wanted to help, didn't I . . .' I can feel my cheeks burning up.

'Delilah, don't be so rude,' says Florence. 'Come in, all of you, please. It really is very kind of you.'

'This is my dad and my nana, Nana Sparrow.'

'You've brought your whole family!' says Delilah.

'Delilah! Manners! They have come to make our flat a home. Go and get the biscuit tin, and put the kettle on. Now!'

'Delilah, you can call me Nana Sparrow – all the kids round Camden do.'

As Florence leads Dad and Nana Sparrow through a door into their front room, I remain standing on the doorstep feeling a fool.

'Well, are you coming in or not?' says Delilah.

'Don't mind,' I say.

'Suit yourself,' she says, and wanders into what I guess is her bedroom.

I feel so big and awkward, and I am not sure what to do . . . so I follow her.

'About yesterday . . .' she says. 'I thought maybe you were coming to check up on me.'

'Well, would it have been so bad if I had?' I say. 'That's what friends do.'

Delilah does that sideways glance of hers, through her eyelashes.

'Do you want to see my reading den?' she asks.

I follow her to the corner of her bedroom where there is a big tepee tent made out of a huge Jamaican flag.

Delilah undoes the tapes that tie the entrance shut, and disappears inside it. I squash myself in but I am too big. My knees are by my ears and my head is bowed over.

It's a properly amazing den – a place for sharing secrets. My Moon Dog mystery nearly comes popping out of my mouth. I am busting to tell Delilah but in my gut I'm thinking, *Keep it to yourself, just till you know more*. I bite my lip and look around me, drinking in the details.

The inside walls of the tepee are made from white sheets. Delilah is sitting cross-legged on a huge purple cushion, surrounded by piles of books. Behind her is a painting of a sunflower. *A Child Needs Books to Grow Like a Flower Needs Water* is painted underneath. Going round the walls are beautiful drawings of the London Eye, St Paul's Cathedral and the Tower of London, just like her keyrings. Above St Paul's Cathedral are painted the words, *Great things come in small packages*.

'Wow!' I say, 'cause I've never seen nothing like this before.

'My dad made it for me,' she says. 'It's my hideout from the world. He used to say, it's to remind me where I come from and that I am a unique, special young lady who will find my way in the world and I must never forget that.'

'Your dad . . .'

'He's dead,' she says.

'You needed Wilbur,' I say.

Delilah looks at me and smiles and I just know that being her friend is the most important thing in the world to me.

'I get sad about Mum,' I say.

'Is she dead?'

'No, she went off with her boyfriend Luke, to find herself, she reckoned. Only I think she forgot she had a son.'

'Oh,' says Delilah, giving my arm the quickest of squeezes.

'Room for another little one?' says Nana Sparrow, lying on her belly and pushing her head through the opening.

'Oh, my word! Now, this is really special, Delilah. Your mum says, did you get the biscuits, 'cause she can't find them in the kitchen cupboard?'

Delilah giggles, puts her finger in front of her lips.

'Don't tell,' she says, reaching behind a pile of books and pulling out a biscuit tin in the shape of a red London bus. 'I'd better go and give them to Mum.'

We all wander through to the front room and crash on the sofa, dunking chocolate digestives into hot sweet tea. Florence brings in Nana Sparrow's heated-up apple pie and we have a slice of that too. I am watching my dad whistling while he works, as he puts up shelves and then a curtain rail.

'Do you need any help, Dad?' I ask.

'No, it's OK, son. You have a nice time with your friend. It's good to see you enjoying yourself.'

It's funny, 'cause I was just thinking the exact same thing: how good it is to see my dad enjoying his work.

'Let's go and get your kitchen sorted,' says Nana, pulling Florence off the sofa.

Delilah leads me back to her bedroom. In the corner is a pile of old vinyl records, and a proper old record player.

'These were my dad's,' says Delilah. 'He loved his music, and Mum said he had such eclectic taste. He loved R&B and soul but he also loved his musicals.'

She picks out an album called *Saturday Night Fever*, and she carefully puts the needle on one of the tracks. Catchy music fills the bedroom. The men singing have these really high voices. It's a song about jive talking. Whatever that is.

And before I know it, Delilah and me are dancing and snapping our fingers in time to the music. My dog lead falls out of my pocket. Snatching it up off the carpet, I swing it around and start making up my own words to the song.

'*We are le le le lead walking*

Though we ain't got a dog

Lead walking through the park and the bog

We are lead walking

We are telling no lies

Lead walking the dogs in disguise . . .'

Then Delilah grabs her dog lead from the back of her wardrobe, and we are dancing backwards and forwards, swinging our dog leads in time to the music.

I turn round, and Dad is standing in the doorway laughing, a drill in his hand.

'Come and see this, Mum,' he shouts and Florence and Nana Sparrow watch us as we sing and dance, and as they applaud us, I think it's the most fun I have ever had.

'Back to work,' says Nana Sparrow as Delilah and I flop on her bed, tired after all that dancing.

When all the adults have gone back to their chores, Delilah closes her bedroom door and whispers, 'Guess what? I think Mum might get me a puppy.'

'What, she actually said that?' I say. Happy daydreams zap my brain of Delilah and me, walking her dog on the heath.

'She said she's not promising anything, so that's not a no.'

'Oh, so that's an almost puppy,' I say.

'Yes, definitely an almost puppy,' she says.

Delilah switches on her laptop and we scroll through adverts of puppies. Words like *teacup* and *miniature* jump out at us, and Delilah is awwwwing and oooohing beside me. A photograph of four Cavalier pups sitting on a white sheepskin rug. **PUPPIES FROM GOOD FAMILY HOME. CALL IVAN**, says the advert, followed by a mobile phone number. A photo of pug puppies sitting in an armchair in front of a pink wall. **PUPPIES FROM MOTHER, WHO IS A MUCH-LOVED FAMILY PET**, says the advert. **CALL BARRY**. French bulldog puppies playing on a yellow rug, with stripy wallpaper in the background. **CALL ALVIN**. And on and on, puppies upon puppies upon puppies.

'Oh, oh, oh, look, Marcus, look at their little faces.' Delilah is gushing over a photo of six of the tiniest dachshund puppies. The little dachshunds are sitting in a row on a yellow sofa. **VIEW PUPPIES WITH MOTHER, FULL PAPERWORK PROVIDED**, says the advert. **CALL GEORGE**.

'I'm going to show Mum,' says Delilah, running out of her bedroom with her laptop.

I hear Florence shouting from the kitchen. 'DELILAH! THIS IS NOT THE TIME TO TALK ABOUT PUPPIES, WHEN I AM BALANCING ON A STOOL, REACHING FOR THE TOP CUPBOARD.'

I hear Nana Sparrow's loud laugh. Delilah runs back into the bedroom, clutching her laptop and a handful of chocolate digestives.

'I am sure that's a nearly yes,' she says, giggling and shoving three biscuits into my hand.

She is so happy she is practically flying round the bedroom, but choosing a puppy is such a

71

life-changing decision. Matt the Vet told us this when he came to Heath Academy to do his talk. I need to bring Delilah back down to earth and give her a proper dog talk.

'Delilah,' I say, 'please do not get carried away with cute pictures on the Internet.'

'How do you mean?' She gives me a funny look.

'Well, um . . .' *Choose you words proper careful, Marcus*, I think to myself. 'What I'm trying to say, is that before you buy a puppy, you need to meet the mother dog, and see the pups, and pick the right one for you.' I try to remember Matt the Vet's words. 'It's a big decision, and you've got to be strong enough to walk away if none of them are right for you. You have to do it properly. Not go falling in love with some photo on the Internet.'

'People do their food shopping online all the time,' says Delilah.

'A puppy is not a vegetable, it's a living, breathing animal, Delilah.'

She gives me a funny look.

'Are you jealous?'

'No! Delilah, I am not jealous, all right. I'm just trying to be real.' And so that she really believes me I blurt, 'Anyhow, I've got something better than an almost puppy to tell you.' And I can't stop my words as they come running out of my mouth. 'I've met an actual, definite dog, the most beautiful black Newfoundland you ever did see. I've named him Moon Dog.'

'Moon Dog,' repeats Delilah, as if she's tasting the words. 'That's a wondrous name.'

'Oh, Delilah, I just hope I see him again, so that he has love in his dog life, and I have dog love in my life, 'cause his owners haven't even got a name for him. They just call him Dog.'

Delilah's face screws up with anger.

'Tell me everything,' she says.

'Go in your book den, it's a good place for secrets and the grown-ups must not hear. If they poke their noses in, Moon Dog might disappear with his owners and I want to help him. I've gotta get him to trust me.'

She jumps off her bed, leaps across her

bedroom and ducks into her tepee book-den. I follow her, scrunching myself in a ball, and whisper words of Moon Dog and of Nose Ring and Leopard Tattoo moving furniture in the middle of the night, and I'm just telling her about the box of mobile phones when Nana Sparrow pokes her head through the tepee entrance and stops my secret.

'Time to go,' she says.

'Delilah,' I say, 'shall we go lead walking on the heath tomorrow?'

'Yes.' She nods.

'Meet me on the corner of my road, Mabel Street, outside Grayson & Stoat estate agents at twelve,' I say, and life feels good.

As Dad drives down Mabel Street in the dusk, at the end of the street I see three shadowy figures in a row, leaning against our wall, waiting. When I get out of the van, Nico, Sol and Baz leap off the garden wall, sending the bins clattering, and walk slowly towards me.

My 'life is good' feeling shatters all over the pavement.

7

Marcus

Nico smiles a smarmy grin.

'Allow me, Mrs Sparrow.' And takes the box that Nana is lifting out of the back of our van.

'OK then, if you insist. If you could take it up the path and put it on my doorstep, there's a good lad.'

'No, I'll take it,' I say, reaching for the box.

Nico kicks me in the shin.

Dad locks the van and comes round to join us.

Sol says, 'Good evening, Mr Sparrow, and how are you all this fine day?'

My thoughts scramble. What are they up to? Why are they talking like this?

Nico shoves Baz in the back.

'We was wondering, Mr Sparrow, as it's such a nice evening, if Marcus would like to come on a walk with us?'

No, no, this can't happen. If I start hanging out with the Cinder Street Boyz, Delilah will de-friend me. She will not want to know me, it's a fact.

'No, I can't, sorry, 'cause I'm grounded. I gotta pick all my clothes off my bedroom floor. Isn't that right, Nana?'

Please, Nana Sparrow, please, make me tidy my bedroom. Make me tidy it please, please, please, I say over and over, inside my head.

Nana's face is all screwed up, and she's giving them one of her looks.

'Aren't you the boys we drove past and saw making a nuisance of yourselves outside the shops this morning?'

Baz smirks and Nico punches him in the arm, shoving him out of the way.

'No, it weren't us, we would never do such a thing, would we, boys?'

'No, no, no. Not us. Never,' they chorus.

'Oh, go on, Marcus. I'll let you off tidying your bedroom. You are only young once.'

Nico carries the box up the garden path and leaves it on the doorstep for Nana. 'Thank you,' she says. 'It's nice to see a bit of manners. Have a nice time, lads.'

'Bye, Mrs Sparrow,' they all call.

As soon as Nana's inside, Nico shoves me in the back.

'Avoiding us, are you?'

'No,' I say.

'We've seen you with your little girlfriend,' says Sol.

'She's not my girlfriend, she's a friend.'

'Bit small for you, ain't she? You might stamp on her by accident,' says Baz.

They all laugh.

I feel my anger-match light.

'Look at his face. Missing Mummy, are you?' says Sol.

The flame flares up. I step towards Sol's grinning face. I don't care about anything. I just want to hurt him.

Nico laughs and flings his arm round my shoulder.

'Whoa! That's why we want you hanging round with us, see. You've got balls.' And before I know it, my anger has reached my feet, and I am running through the street with them, whooping and hollering.

People cross over to the other side of the road to keep away from us, and it feels good.

Baz smashes a bottle that's balancing on a wall on to the pavement, and I start kicking the tiny pieces of glass into the drain, because I don't want a dog to cut its paws. But Sol yanks me away, and we are off again. Kicking lamp posts, shouting, running into the Sainsbury's car park. I jump into a trolley and Nico jumps into another one, and Sol and Baz charge the trolleys into each other again and again, clashing metal on metal. Mine tips over and I scramble out, scraping my knee.

'Oi, you runts!'

I turn my head, and a security guard is running towards us, shaking his fist. Off we go again, sprinting out of the car park, kicking cans, jumping on walls, and my anger explodes, and it feels good, like I belong.

And we are on the heath, running up a hill towards the burnt ruins of Rose Manor Hall, ragged and menacing against the darkening sky. We stop.

'They say if you listen hard when the wind's blowing, you can hear the whimpering of the ghost children what used to live there,' says Nico.

'Yeah, a boy and a girl, they arrived home from boarding school in olden day Victorian times, in their horse and carriage, and their house was on fire. They just stood and whimpered, as their home burned down,' says Sol.

My bones shiver.

'Tell him, go on, tell him what his initiation into the Cinder Street Boyz is,' says Baz, hopping from one foot to the other.

Sol grabs my ear and hisses into it, pointing to a burnt brick wall towering in front of us.

'You gotta smash this wall up. That is your initiation into the Cinder Street Boyz, you gotta make it crumble.'

I swallow. 'When?' But a police siren cuts through the air.

'Run,' shouts Baz, and we all scarper.

'We'll let you know when,' shouts Nico, over his shoulder.

The flame inside me fizzles out as I walk home, and I don't feel good, and I don't feel strong. I feel really, really stupid if the truth be known.

A cold breeze swirls round me. I think of meeting Delilah tomorrow and smile a secret smile. We are going *lead walking*. Then a sliver of cold dread lurches in my belly. Why would Delilah want to be friends with an idiot people cross the road to get away from? I hate myself, to be honest. I don't want to do an initiation ceremony. I don't want to hang around with the Cinder Street Boyz. I just want to be friends with Delilah.

The FOR SALE sign has tipped over the wall

again but I can't even be bothered to haul it back up.

I let myself in. Nana is in the kitchen.

'I've made you some sausages and chips,' she says, plonking the plate in front of me.

'Thanks,' I say. 'Where's Dad?'

'He's gone back to bed,' she mutters and the sadness inside me shatters my heart. Nana Sparrow looks so sorrowful as she wanders through to the front room and switches on the TV.

Heavy with chips, I plod out into the back garden and sit on my wooden crate-seat. It starts to get darker and colder, but I don't care.

A cold, wet nose pushes itself through the hole in the fence. Moon Dog is back! I hold out my palm and Moon Dog rests his warm, furry chin in my hand, and this time it stays there.

8

Delilah

I am waiting for Marcus on the corner of Mabel Street, outside Grayson & Stoat estate agents, like he said. It's Sunday, so it's closed, but a light seeping under a door at the back of the office catches my eye.

'DELILAH.' A shout bounces towards me.

It's Marcus walking down Mabel Street and he looks like he's even combed his hair!

A quick check of my reflection in the window: I inspect my new jeans and favourite red trainers, and slightly unzip my massive parka with the big furry hood. I adjust the red beanie on my head, flicking my hair behind my shoulders.

'Looking good, Delilah,' I say to myself as I smile at my reflection.

'Hi,' he says, grinning. 'Ready?' And we do

that awkward not-quite-knowing-whether-to-hug-each-other thing, but then we don't and we cross the road.

Suddenly, Marcus grabs my arm and pulls me behind a tree.

'Delilah, look,' he whispers, and points towards Grayson & Stoat. 'It's him, one of the men I saw moving furniture next door in the middle of the night.'

Peeping through the branches, I see a man inside the estate agents with spiky gelled hair.

'Look at his tattoo!' Marcus whispers.

I look at the man's rolled-up shirtsleeves which show off a dazzling leopard tattooed on his arm. You can't miss it.

'So Leopard-Tattoo Man is an estate agent,' I whisper. 'That's why he's at the house. Maybe Moon Dog is his and he just brings his dog to work, takes him to the houses he's showing people round?'

'In the middle of the night?' whispers Marcus.

Leopard-Tattoo Man looks either way before stepping out through the door on to the street. He obviously doesn't want to be seen. He is followed by that rude boy from school, Nico, the one who thinks he's really something. He has what looks like a banknote screwed up in his fist.

'That's the second time I've seen Nico at the estate agents with money in his hand,' whispers Marcus. 'What's he doing there?'

Leopard-Tattoo Man walks over to a car parked outside and opens the boot. There's a small cardboard box at the back. Nico struts off round the corner, disappearing into Cinder Street.

Marcus is chewing his lip, looking properly puzzled.

'Come on,' I say. 'They've gone. I want to make the most of my freedom. My mum literally tried everything to stop me coming out. She even bribed me with licking out the bowl from the strawberry cupcakes she's baking, like I'm three or something.'

'Nana Sparrow made me pick up stuff from my bedroom floor, but then practically booted me out of the door,' says Marcus. 'She says she wants me out of her hair for the afternoon.'

Marcus looks down and shuffles his feet, looking shy, which I've gotta say is properly sweet. 'Nana Sparrow likes you a lot, thinks you'll be a good influence on me.' Then he looks up and grins.

'Ready?' I grin back, and we take off, swinging our leads and singing our song.

And I'm feeling good in my new jeans and trainers.

'We are le le le lead walking . . .

Though we ain't got a dog—'

My phone bleeps.

A text from Mum.

Please come home.

I text back:

No Mum

And continue singing our song.

'Lead walking through the park and the bog

We are lead walking—'

My phone bleeps again.

DELILAH PLEASE.

I ignore the text and carry on singing.

'We are telling no lies

Lead walking the dogs in disguise . . .'

We walk across the grass and come to a part of the lake fenced off especially for dogs. In the water, two dalmatians are swimming towards the same stick that has been thrown for them. A Cavalier King

Charles is standing on the bank, looking as if he can't decide whether to go for a swim, and a chocolate Labrador emerges from the pond right by where we stand and starts shaking her coat. Marcus and I jump out of the way just in time, as sprays of water hit a lady in a blue coat next to us carrying a pug who squeals.

'Oh, Marcus, this is totally brilliant. I never knew about this dog pond.'

Marcus nudges me and says, 'One day it'll be us bringing our dogs here to swim.' And we give each other a high-five.

We continue singing our song as we walk towards Rose Manor Hall. I remember the story about the ghost children. Everyone is talking about it. When I was in the medical room, drinking my lemonade with Miss Raquel, I could hear Nico talking at the top of his voice outside in the corridor, saying how if you listen hard you can hear the ghost children whimpering. Miss Raquel got vexed with him, told him to get back to his class and stop talking nonsense.

I've not been here before, though. Dad would

have loved it; he treasured nature. I run ahead, to stop the sad wave drowning me. When I look back, Marcus has stopped in his tracks.

'Come on, Delilah, I don't want to go up to Rose Manor Hall. We can explore over there.' He points to a patch of trees on the horizon.

'Oh, Marcus,' I laugh, 'scared of the ghost children, are you?'

'No,' says Marcus, puffing up his chest. 'I'm not scared of anything.'

He runs up the hill to join me, but I need to catch my breath so we walk up the rest of the way. It takes us ages, because we have to say hello to every single dog we see as we trudge up the hill: a golden retriever, a greyhound, a bulldog and two Staffies.

Eventually, we reach the very top. The beauty of the place catches my breath.

'Delilah,' says Marcus, 'we've seen it now, let's go, it's just old and dead.'

'Marcus, use your eyes. This place is so alive. It's magical, in such a sad, lost way. A house that, I reckon, was once so full of love, now long forgotten.'

Marcus slowly smiles as he looks around him,

and I just know that he is seeing it through my eyes for the very first time. We run around laughing, stretching out to touch the roses and honeysuckle, following their paths with our fingers as far as we can, as they wind round and round and up, up, up, tall wooden posts and crumbling walls that tower way above my head. A red admiral butterfly lands on the honeysuckle, just by my cheek. I hold my breath as it gathers nectar, then off it flutters. A tiny little field mouse scurries over my foot. It's so cute.

'Marcus, be careful,' I say, shoving him out of the way. I don't want him stamping on the tiny mouse with his big foot.

My phone bleeps. Another text from Mum.

Don't fall into a puddle. x

I am not even going to answer that one. It hasn't even been raining!

'This can be our place,' I say, 'where we can walk our dogs when we get them.'

Marcus's cheeks have gone rosy red.

'Yes, our dogs will love sniffing around the ruins and we can come here, and no one will find us, and we can share secrets and stuff,' he gabbles.

'It's our wondrous place,' I say, and just then a gust of wind blows my hair in my eyes, and I am sure I hear whimpering.

'Listen,' I say, putting my hand on Marcus's arm, but all is silent.

Then the faint sounds of dogs barking far, far away.

A chaffinch flies on to the top of the broken wall and tweeps at us.

Dad used to call me his little chaffinch.

My memory is broken as Sol steps out from behind the wall. Nico is standing on one side of him and the dozy-looking boy, Baz, on the other.

Marcus is looking down at the grass and acting weird.

'Can I help you?' I say.

'You're on our territory,' says the dozy one.

'Yeah, you tell 'em, Baz,' says Nico, stepping right up in my face.

'Why, why is it yours?' I say. 'Where's your names? Are they written on the walls, the grass, the sky? No. I don't think so. Stop with your nonsense. It's bad enough I gotta see your ugly faces at school, without seeing them on a Sunday.'

Marcus pulls at my arm. 'Delilah, leave it. Come away.'

'No, I'm—'

'Please, Delilah.' And there is this look in his eye, which, for once in my life, makes me shut my big mouth, and I walk down the hill with him.

'We'll be having words with you, Big M,' shouts Nico, 'but leave your little girlfriend at home next time.'

We carry on down the hill, no words said, but my thoughts are ticking over.

'Marcus, what do they mean, *they'll be having words with you*, and why are they calling you Big M, like you're some hard boy in their gang?'

'They don't mean nothing. They're just chatting rubbish. Look, Delilah, I know you're brave and well . . . you're tremendous. But please don't mess with them boys.'

'They don't scare me, Marcus.'

'They should do. They scare me. I know you can look after yourself, but I would never ever forgive myself if anything happened to you when you were with me.'

And Marcus looks so red in the face and properly awkward that I just break all my rules about not kissing boys. I do a massive leap in the air and give him a smacker on the cheek, and before things get too soppy I shout, 'Race you to the tree.'

I win easy 'cause I'm fast, and Marcus is lumbering behind.

My phone bleeps a text.

Do not climb trees. You might fall.

Cupcakes nearly ready . . .

I start to climb the tree.

Marcus follows. We sit straddling the biggest, longest branch, facing each other.

'I've got something for you, Marcus.' And I dig in my pocket and bring out my old phone.

'There you go, I got an upgrade. It works most of the time. Giving it a shake usually does the trick. It's got lots of cool pictures of dogs on it. Look.'

'I don't know what to say, Delilah.'

'Just take it.'

He grins and starts to flick through the pictures. It feels so good to make Marcus happy like this.

Every time I try and talk to him, my phone bleeps.
My mum is seriously annoying.

Come home.

Bleep.

**I don't want you to catch cold.
It's going to be dark soon.**

Bleep.

Come home, you can have a puppy.

'Yahoooo,' I cry. 'Yes, yes, yes, yes, yes,' I shout,
showing Marcus my text.

We hold our arms up in the air, and shout at the
top of our voices, 'WE ARE TREMENDOUS,' and the
wind swirls round us, and I am sure I hear dogs
barking, though it's strange 'cause there's not one
dog to be seen.

Our part of the heath is quite, quite empty.

'Time to go home and eat strawberry cupcakes,'
I say.

9

Marcus

Delilah is coming to my house for tea tonight! But first, we are in trouble at school.

Big trouble.

Me and Delilah are sitting in a 'neither of you have been concentrating in any of your lessons' detention. But how are you meant to concentrate in your lessons when you have major dog issues?

Yesterday evening, after lead walking on the heath with Delilah, I ran home all the way to Mabel Street. I held on to the Saturday-night memory of Moon Dog resting his chin in my hand for the longest time. But Moon Dog wasn't there.

Maybe he's only there at night, I thought, so

I set my phone alarm to vibrate under my pillow every hour so I could look out of my window to check if he was there. But the garden lay empty. And no sign of Nose Ring and Leopard Tattoo either. Where is he? Where is my Moon Dog?

As for Delilah, the girl is obsessed with getting a puppy. She hasn't given it a rest, not once today.

Miss Raquel doesn't know I have a phone now, and Delilah used her saved-up pocket money to put credits on a pay-as-you-go SIM for me – but she is using up all the credits looking at puppy adverts under the desk.

We've had geography puppy, maths puppy, English puppy – while I have spent my lessons missing Moon Dog, and dreaming about me and Delilah walking a proper real-life puppy. I got told off three times in maths for singing 'Lead Walking'.

We spent lunchtime in the library to make sure we'd be on time for Wilbur, who was due to come in. Also, the library is a good place to hide from the Cinder Street Boyz, as Baz, Sol and Nico do not read books.

'Marcus Sparrow,' Mrs Johnson said, 'it is my mission to get you to read something without the word "dog" in the title. There is a whole world of beautiful books out there, just waiting for you to discover. *And when are you going to bring back the books you borrowed, please?*'

'Soon, Mrs Johnson, soon,' I said. 'I told you I got that reluctance thing and I should be in that reader's group so I can read to Wilbur, instead of going to maths.' At which point Mrs Johnson snorted with laughter and gave us a custard cream each from her secret stash.

Just as we were scoffing them down, I heard a snuffling behind me. Wilbur was pulling the lady with the red hair into the library.

'Ah, Marnie, right on time,' said Mrs Johnson.

'Pleased to meet you, Marnie,' I said, grabbing her hand and pumping it up and down in a firm handshake.

Nana Sparrow always says it's good to learn people's names and be polite.

Delilah was already on the floor with her

arms round Wilbur, rolling around with him on the library carpet.

Not letting go of Marnie's hand, I said, 'Please can I be of assistance to Wilbur and yourself, so that you can put your feet up and have a nice cup of tea with Mrs Johnson.'

'Marcus, Marcus, Marcus,' said Mrs Johnson, laughing and shoving the dog bowl into my other hand. 'Go on then, show me you are a responsible young man and get Wilbur a nice drink of water. It is your special duty, do not let me down.'

Proud of my special duty, I made my way to the playground and weaved myself through all the lunchtime games of football. Kids were shouting at me to get out of the way but I ignored them all – even when a ball bounced off my head and scored a goal! – and made it to the water fountain to fill Wilbur's bowl.

As I carried the bowl of water, carefully, carefully, back across the playground, a ball hit me hard in the back, jolting me so I spilled the water down my front. I turned round to find Sol, Nico and Baz standing in front of me in a line. Nico poked me hard in the chest with his finger.

'Are you hiding from us, Big M?'

'No, I'm busy. Got a special duty to perform.'

'A special duty,' said Baz, snatching the bowl and throwing the rest of the water in my face.

'IDIOTS!' bellowed Delilah, who had come hurtling across the playground. 'The dog needs a drink.' She snatched the bowl back to fill it up again.

'Who are you calling an idiot, little girl?' said Sol.

'Well, you must know it's your name or you wouldn't have answered,' said Delilah. 'Mrs Johnson is waiting for you, Marcus.' She stormed back through the playground. I had to run to catch her up.

'Soon, Big M, soon,' shouted Sol after us.

'What do they mean, *soon*, Marcus?' asked Delilah.

'They said I gotta play football with them soon,' I lied, feeling sick about doing the gang initiation and Delilah de-friending me for sure.

'I am telling you, Marcus, stay away from the Cinder Street Boyz.'

And Delilah's warning has been banging around in my brain all day and my uniform still feels damp as I sit next to her in detention now.

Delilah and I have been given a piece of paper each, as we are meant to be doing an essay called '*Why I Must Learn to Concentrate*'. Which is so unfair, 'cause I reckon I *am* concentrating hard, thinking about Moon Dog, and Delilah is most definitely concentrating on getting a puppy.

Mr Burnett, who is on detention duty, is drawing in his sketchbook. I don't think he takes his detention duties very seriously. He hasn't even noticed that Delilah has drawn lots of little dogs and hearts with 'I love sausage dogs', which is another name for dachshunds, all over her essay paper and is now looking at a picture of some dachshund puppies on my phone, which she is hiding under the desk. And instead of doing my '*Why I Must Learn to*

Concentrate' essay, I am thinking about what it would be like if Moon Dog was my own dog. I start to draw out a plan on my piece of paper as I think about the key hidden underneath my top thinking crate, and wonder when I will get the chance to explore next door again and see Moon Dog.

My Moon Dog Training Plan

Tricks that I want him to learn:

Sit

Lie down

Roll

Fetch

High-five

Things to do with Moon Dog:

1. Bus rides round London – to get him used to public transport for his ~~soculization~~ socialisation skills

2. Swimming in the dog pond at Parliament Hill – if I take Moon Dog to the dog pond at

Parliament Hill I will have to remember to take spare towels to give to people if Moon Dog shakes his coat next to them or covers them with thick gooey dribble drool. Newfoundlands are brilliant at swimming and have webbed feet and a thick coat to keep warm in freezing water. They can be trained to rescue people and pull them to safety

3. Walks to our place, Rose Manor Hall – Moon Dog can have a good sniff around the ~~ruins~~ ruins while I have my secret chats with Delilah

4. Trips to the seaside. We can drive up in the Sparrow's Fruit & Veg Van. Though this will need Nana Sparrow. Maybe trips could be ~~negotieated~~ negotiated if I tidied my bedroom

I am concentrating so hard that I am surprised when Mr Burnett announces, 'Right you two, the evening is young, and waiting for you to explore, go, now.' He forgets to ask us for our essays, which is brilliant 'cause we would be in even more trouble if we had to give in our pieces of paper.

'Goodbye, Sir,' we shout, grabbing our bags and racing for the door.

'Good night, Marcus and Delilah. Dream big,' he calls after us.

'We will, Sir,' I call back, 'cause if you ask me, Moon Dog is a very big dream.

A ginormous one in fact.

'Freedom!' says Delilah, jumping high in the air. 'So amazing Mum's gone to her cousin Rosemary's, 'cause she'd have never let me come to you otherwise.'

We sing 'Lead Walking' all the way across the playground, along Cinder Street and down Mabel Street.

'What's for tea?' says Delilah. 'I'm star—'

I grab her arm.

'Delilah, look.'

The FOR SALE sign outside next door has gone, and a tall, skinny woman in a red dress is walking down the path carrying a cardboard box. I want to ask her if she's bought the house and what's in her box and I know that's nosy and rude and Nana Sparrow would *kill me* for asking a stranger questions, but I don't care. I'm just crossing the road to speak to her, when our front door swings open and Nana Sparrow marches down the path.

'YOU ARE LATE. AND DELILAH, YOUR MUM'S JUST BEEN ON THE PHONE ASKING IF YOU GOT HERE SAFELY!'

'Sorry, Nana Sparrow,' says Delilah, running up to her and giving her a hug. She is *so* smooth. 'We got detention, our teachers are so unfair . . .' I can hear Delilah chatting on to Nana.

By this time the woman in the red dress has gone.

I dawdle behind them, feeling sick. If Leopard-Tattoo Man has sold the house to the lady in the red dress I won't see Moon Dog again, not ever, and I can't bear it. My tummy rumbles and I feel empty with sadness.

Nana Sparrow is in her cauliflower stage. We had cauliflower on toast for breakfast and as I walk into the house, the yummy smell of cauliflower cheese wafts up my nose – but my Moon Dog sadness has stolen my appetite.

'There's been comings and goings next door,' Nana Sparrow tells us once we've washed our hands and sat down at the table. 'Banging and thumping and I'm sure I heard a dog barking.' She dollops big helpings of cauliflower and cheese on to our plates. 'I think they must have sold Mr Anderson's house. It's about time.'

'A dog!' Delilah looks across at me.

I kick her under the table. 'Did you see the dog, Nana?' I ask.

'No, I haven't got time to go looking for dogs. I was trying to add up my stall takings, driving me mad the noise was. I couldn't think.'

So Moon Dog was next door when I was stuck at school.

I can't believe I missed him.

The doorbell rings.

'That'll be Alf, he said he'd call round for his window cleaning money. Give him that with my thanks,' says Nana Sparrow, shoving a brown envelope in my hand.

Alf might have Flora, his Staffie, with him. I run to open the front door to reveal Alf and Flora on the other side. I fling myself down on my knees to get Staffie kisses to try and ease the ache in my heart. I drop the envelope and Flora snatches it in her mouth, and Alf and I are laughing, trying to make her drop it, and she does. I get to my feet to give the wet, soggy, chewed-up mess of an envelope to Alf and that's when I see it. The FOR SALE sign is back in next door's garden.

I just gape at it.

'What's the matter, lad?' asks Alf.

'Nothing.' I shove the envelope into his hand. 'Maybe you could iron the money, Alf,' I say. 'Goodbye and thank you.'

Shutting the front door, I race back to the dinner table and the steaming-hot plates of cauliflower cheese.

'The For Sale sign's back up,' I say, catching Delilah's eye. 'Looks like nobody's bought it.'

Nana Sparrow sighs. 'Never known a house

be empty for so long.'

Suddenly I'm starving, knowing there's a chance I might see my Moon Dog again.

'Smells good,' says Delilah, and for someone so small, she can't half eat.

'What?' says Delilah, seeing me gape at her. 'I'm a growing girl.'

'I'll take some up to Dad,' I say, thinking he might even ask me about my day at school if he's hungry for his dinner.

I clutch the tray with both hands, determined not to drop it, and kick the door open with my foot.

'Hello, Dad,' I say, carrying the tray into his room.

He doesn't even look at me.

'It's proper tasty,' I try again.

Nothing.

'I got detention at school today, Dad, for not concentrating,' I say, willing him to tell me off.

I count to ten slowly in my head but still nothing.

I leave the tray on his bedside table.

'Enjoy your dinner, Dad,' I say and run out of the room and all the way down the stairs.

After supper, we play Monopoly. I lay the board on the table and hold all the silver tokens out in my hand for Delilah and Nana to pick, hoping I get to be the dog.

Delilah reaches for the top hat.

'No one can be the hat,' she says quietly, putting it back in the box. 'That's what my dad always was when we played on Sundays. He said the top hat had style, like him on the dance floor. I'll be the dog.'

I let her without even arguing, 'cause I don't want Delilah to be sad.

'I'll be the iron,' says Nana Sparrow, 'because that's all I seem to spend my days doing. You can be the boot, Marcus, 'cause you've got big feet.'

We all laugh and start our game. Nana Sparrow keeps helping herself to money from the bank.

'You can't do that, Nana,' I say, 'it's cheating.'

'No it's not,' she says. 'I'm the one that does

the shopping in this house, so it stands to reason that I'm the one who needs the money.'

'That's not the rules of the game, Nana Sparrow,' I complain, with my head in my hands. But there's no telling her, and the game ends up a shambles with Nana somehow managing to send me and Delilah to jail at the same time by evicting us from the houses she owns in Mayfair for not tidying our bedrooms or paying her enough rent. We are not even on the Mayfair square. I am on Liverpool Street and Delilah is on Marylebone, so that isn't even a rule of the game. Nana Sparrow reckons she somehow owns the whole of London. I am just about to tell her off for cheating, when I catch her looking at Delilah, who has rolled out of the chair, she is laughing so much. Nana Sparrow has a spark in her eye, and I realise she has done the whole thing to distract Delilah from her dad sadness. I love my Nana Sparrow.

We laugh till our bellies ache. Then I have a memory flash of playing Monopoly with my mum and dad when I was about five, and it feels like I am being punched.

I look up and Delilah is staring at me.

'Think of today, not yesterdays. All the yesterdays have gone,' she says.

'How did you . . .'

'I can see it in your eyes,' she says, and yawns.

The phone rings. Nana snatches it up.

'Yes . . . Yes, of course she can stay . . . No trouble. Hello? Hello? Oh, we've been cut off.'

Nana puts the phone down.

'Your mum's train's been cancelled, there's been a signal failure, she's no way of getting home so you're stopping here for the night.'

Delilah's phone starts bleeping with about a million texts.

She shows them to me and rolls her eyes.

Behave.

I'll pick you up for your dentist appointment in the morning.

Clean your teeth.

Have a glass of water before bed.

'Time for bed,' says Nana, and she irons one of my T-shirts from the ironing pile.

'Wear this to sleep in.' She holds it in front of Delilah.

'It's like a dress on you,' I say.

Delilah shrugs her shoulders.

Nana makes Delilah a bed on the sofa.

'I know I've got a spare toothbrush somewhere,' she says, disappearing upstairs.

'It's been a good evening,' says Delilah.

'The very best,' I say. 'Good night, Delilah.'

'Night, Marcus.'

I tumble into bed and must have fallen asleep straight away, but something wakes me from my dreams. I go to the window and open my curtain.

Moon Dog is in next door's garden and he is looking up at me.

10

Delilah

I am shaken awake by Marcus hissing in my ear.

'Wake up. Moon Dog's back. Come on, he's waiting for us.'

I pull on my school trousers under Marcus's T-shirt. I've got a feeling that going to see Moon Dog will involve me being hoisted over next door's fence, and I don't want Marcus to see my knickers. I feel for my shoes in the dark – no time for socks – and follow Marcus out.

He leads me down to the bottom of the garden, to a pile of crates by the fence.

Clambering up them, I stand on tiptoes to peep over the fence and gasp.

Moon Dog is looking up at me, and words cannot describe the instant love I feel for this magnificent dog.

'I am going to get the quilt off my bed,' says Marcus. 'Look, he's only got that dirty old towel to sleep on.'

I see a turned-over dog bowl on the grass, halfway down the garden.

'Lift me over the fence first and bring some fresh water out. Moon Dog's kicked his bowl over.'

'Will you be all right?' says Marcus.

'Of course I will! Get on with it. We need to take this opportunity to get him to trust us.'

Marcus puts his hand under my armpits, and, hoisting me over the fence, lowers me slowly, slowly down.

'I'll be back,' he whispers, then disappears.

Moon Dog rushes back to his shelter in the corner and cowers, sad eyes looking at me.

'It's OK, boy,' I whisper. 'I'm not going to hurt you. I'm your new friend Delilah.'

Slowly, slowly I hold my hand out.

'Come on, Moon Dog, come and say hello.'

'Delilah – catch!' Marcus is back. He throws his quilt over the fence, then passes a hairbrush and then a jug of water to me, before he climbs over.

'Come on, Moon Dog,' he whispers, so gently, now standing next to me. 'We won't hurt you.'

And, oh so watchfully, the giant dog walks towards us, getting closer and closer, bit by bit.

He licks my cheek, and then Marcus's hand. Drool hangs from his mouth. He rolls over on his back, and we tickle his lovely, warm, furry tummy.

'He don't feel too thin,' I whisper. 'They are feeding him, at least.'

'It's not enough, though, is it,' whispers Marcus. 'A dog needs love.'

'No, it's not enough,' I say.

'Shhh,' says Marcus. 'The men might hear.'

'Come on, let's give you a drink, Moon Dog,' I whisper, righting the dog bowl and filling it with water.

Moon Dog laps it up, then walks with us back to his shelter.

Marcus grabs the water jug and drags the quilt behind him.

'To make it dirty,' he whispers. 'By the look of things, I don't think the men bother to come as far down the garden as Moon Dog's shelter, but if they do, hopefully they will just think it's an old quilt that's blown into the garden from somewhere else.'

I nod and help Marcus spread the quilt out on the rough earth floor of the shelter. I spread the old towel Moon Dog has been sleeping on over the top to hide the quilt a bit.

Moon Dog rolls around on his new bed.

'Do you like that, boy?' whispers Marcus.

'Is that comfier, Moon Dog?' I whisper, kissing him on the top of his head.

'I grabbed Nana Sparrow's hairbrush,' says Marcus, 'I thought you might like to . . .'

'Oh, thank you,' I whisper, taking it from him. I start to gently brush and brush Moon Dog's splendid black fur coat.

Marcus feels down his legs.

'He's got a callous, probably from where he's slept on the hard ground. Poor boy.'

'Maybe we can make the walls of the shelter warmer,' I whisper, grabbing a handful of grass and shoving it in the cracks between the planks of wood.

'That's a brilliant idea,' whispers Marcus. So,

113

under the silver moonlight, Marcus and I pull up tufts and tufts of grass to make Moon Dog's house a home.

The back door crashes open.

We duck, hiding behind Moon Dog.

I shut my eyes and stop breathing.

My head is squashed between Marcus's chest and Moon Dog. I feel Marcus's heart, beating fast. I open my eyes and peep round Moon Dog's back. I see Leopard-Tattoo Man walking closer and closer, shaking a box of dog biscuits.

And do you know what, Moon Dog does not even go to the man, even though he must be hungry. He's keeping us hidden, protecting us, and my love for him grows deeper.

'Come here, you stupid dog,' shouts the man.

Moon Dog growls, a low rumbling growl; he's warning the man to stay away.

Another man's voice calls through the darkness, 'Gary, Fred, Mervin, whatever your name is today,' and laughs, a horrible laugh. 'Come on, we've got to go and get them.'

Leopard-Tattoo Man swears under his breath,

throws a handful of dog biscuits on the grass, and goes back inside.

As soon as the back door slams shut, I quickly hide the hairbrush under the corner of the quilt while Marcus grabs the water jug with one hand and then my hand with the other. I kiss Moon Dog on his head. 'Thank you, Moon Dog,' I whisper and we run to the fence. Marcus climbs over, then reaches down and hoists me up and over after him.

We collapse on the grass, panting, trying to catch our breath.

'What do they mean, *we've got to go and get them*?' whispers Marcus. 'Get what?'

I shrug. 'And why did that other man call Leopard Tattoo by lots of different names?'

'The voice was Nose Ring,' whispers Marcus, 'and I don't know. None of this makes sense.'

Moon Dog sticks his nose through the hole in the fence.

Marcus puts his hand out and Moon Dog's chin rests in it for the longest time.

I whisper, 'Goodbye, you beautiful, beautiful dog. I'll come and see you soon. I love you, Moon Dog.'

11

Marcus

'What do you mean you have lost your quilt?'

The next morning, Nana Sparrow is vexed.

'I don't know. I just woke up and it had gone.'

Well that's not a lie, 'cause when I woke up this morning, it wasn't on my bed, and telling a lie to help a dog isn't a lie in my book.

I am desperate to go to my bedroom window to see if Moon Dog is still there but Nana Sparrow is standing over my bed with her arms folded, giving me one of her *I don't believe you* frowns. She marches me downstairs, still in my PJs and blue towelling dressing gown. I slept in it last night to keep warm in my bed. I hope Moon Dog had a comfortable night with my bed cover.

'This day has not started well,' says Nana Sparrow. 'I cannot find my hairbrush anywhere.' Delilah snorts and turns it into a fake cough. She is already dressed in her school uniform. I look across at her and realise there is mud on the knees of her school trousers, and they are covered in dog hair. I take a big step across the room and stand in front of her. I quickly turn my head and mouth 'knees'. I can hear her brushing them down behind me.

'Mmm,' says Nana Sparrow, 'highly suspicious, if you ask me. You can't just lose a quilt. Right, let's get on with our day. Marcus, watch where you're standing, you're blocking Delilah. And you can stop looking so miserable, you've only got one day of school to get through before half term.'

I realise I'm frowning with the concentration of hiding Delilah brushing her trousers. A small hand digs me in the back. I step out of the way.

'Sorry, Delilah, sorry, Nana Sparrow,' I say. 'I was just thinking about what lessons I've got at school today.'

'Good! You should be thinking about your

book learning. Delilah, if you would like to sit down for breakfast,' says Nana Sparrow and she marches into the kitchen.

'Quick!' Delilah pulls at my dressing gown sleeve, till we are both sitting at the table, then she leans forwards and whispers, 'Marcus, we've gotta keep watch on next door over half term. It's the ideal opportunity. I'm going to try and come over here as much as I can but you know what my mum's like.'

'Moon Dog,' I whisper, holding up my hand for a high-five.

'Moon Dog,' she whispers back, putting her tiny hand flat against mine.

Nana Sparrow brings out a plate, piled high with curious brown lumps, which she then bangs down on the table.

'It's cauliflower fritters. Delilah, what do you usually have for your breakfast?'

'I love a bacon sandwich, Nana Sparrow,' says Delilah.

'One bacon sandwich coming up,' says Nana Sparrow, going back into the kitchen.

'Nana,' I call, 'can I have a bacon sandwich please?'

'No, eat your fritters, Marcus.'

'Yum, yum, Marcus, eat your breakfast,' says Delilah, and I smile at the way she's sitting opposite me with her chin in her hand, eyes twinkling, biting the lip of her rosebud mouth, trying not to laugh.

Rosebud mouth! I'm getting soppy. Though that sounds proper poetic. Delilah does that to me. Now I'm friends with her, I might get good marks in my poetry homework.

I slam back to earth when I take a bite into the yucky-looking things on my plate. They feel slimy and rubbery in my mouth, all at the same time.

The smell of sizzling bacon is filling my taste buds with longing and Delilah is devouring her bacon sandwich to torture me.

'Mmmm, Marcus, this is so deeeelicious, be a good boy and eat up your fritters.'

The doorbell rings and the next moment, Florence flies through the door, suffocating Delilah in a hug as her large bag falls to the floor with a thump.

'I am so sorry, Delilah, there was nothing I could do. I just couldn't get home. Were you OK without me? Gosh, I missed you so much.'

Delilah wriggles free.

'Please, Mum. It was only one night and I had a good time here, a really good time.'

'She was no bother,' says Nana Sparrow, coming out of the kitchen carrying one of her Tupperware boxes. 'Here's some cauliflower cheese for you to heat up for your lunch.'

'That's so thoughtful, thank you for everything,' says Florence, kissing Nana on the cheek.

Delilah takes the cauliflower cheese from Nana Sparrow and unzips Florence's bag to pack it, and as she does, a photo in a frame slides out of the bag.

I hear Delilah make a sharp intake of breath. I see over her shoulder that the photo is of Delilah, and she looks about six. She is sitting on the shoulders of a tall smiling man that must be her dad. The sun is shining and they are standing underneath an apple tree and they are both laughing and young Delilah is reaching up to pick a red shiny apple, only her fingertips can't quite reach.

Delilah sinks to the floor on her knees.

'Rosemary had it framed for you, a happy memory for you to keep.'

Delilah nods and puts the photograph back in the bag. She turns her face away from Florence and Nana, but I see a single tear trickle down her cheek.

'I'll have to invite you all round to ours soon to thank you for all you've done for us,' says Florence. A car beeps. 'That'll be the cab.'

Delilah scurries to gather her things.

'Thank you for having me, Nana Sparrow. See you later, Marcus.'

'Look after Moon Dog,' she whispers to me, and follows her mum down the path.

I wave goodbye as the cab drives away. Delilah looks so tiny and lost in her sadness sitting in the back. I would do anything to bring her happiness back.

As soon as I can, I tear upstairs to look out of

my bedroom window. No sign of Moon Dog, now it's daylight. But I can see my quilt is lying there, under the shelter.

I just hope Nana doesn't look out of my window.

Opening the window as far as it will go, I lean right out so I can look back at next door's house. Nothing, completely deserted. I rush to get washed and dressed.

The FOR SALE sign is still there when I walk past the house to school. With every bone in my body I ache to see my Moon Dog again. I wonder where it is he goes when he is not next door.

Nico, Sol and Baz are waiting for me at the school gate.

'Big M, there you are! Anyone would think you was trying to avoid us.'

'No, I ain't trying to avoid you. I'm just busy,' I say.

'Tonight is the night. Your initiation,' says Sol, poking me in the chest with his knuckles.

'We'll be waiting for you, here at the gate,

after school,' says Nico.

'I got plans for this evening,' I say, my heart hammering.

'Oh, he's got plans. Did you hear him, boys?' says Sol, hissing in my face. 'Well, unplan them. Your initiation's tonight.'

'I've been meaning to tell you ... I don't think I want to be in the Cinder Street Boyz. Thank you for asking me.'

'Big M, mate, you are one of us now,' says Nico. 'You don't have a choice. Or do you want your nana to find out you smashed things up on Saturday night and how the Sainsbury's security guard chased you?'

'Yes, best tell his nana,' says Baz, ''Cause I'm telling you, his dozy dad wouldn't even understand what you was saying.'

The Cinder Street Boyz fall about laughing.

'What did you say?' Before I know it, I've grabbed hold of Baz's shirt collar, my anger match alight. 'My dad ain't dozy . . .'

'Out of the way, boys, you're blocking the entrance,' says Miss Raquel, trying to get past us. 'Marcus, come with me now.'

She walks me to the middle of the playground, away from their ears, and turns to me and says, 'Out with anger, in with love. Come on. You can do it, Marcus.'

I breathe out my anger thoughts of Dad in bed and Baz's cruel, laughing face and what I'd like to do to it, and I breathe in and imagine filling the playground with Moon Dog and Delilah and puppies, puppies everywhere.

'Now, Marcus, are you going to tell me what that was all about?' she asks.

I shake my head. 'It was nothing, Miss.'

'It did not look like nothing to me.'

I keep my mouth shut.

Miss Raquel sighs. 'Well, my door is always open. Do not choose the path of a fight, Marcus, do not go there.'

'No, Miss,' I say. 'I'll help you with your bags.'

The Cinder Street Boyz have caught up with us, and I hear them sniggering behind me. I keep my mouth shut till we get to Miss Raquel's office, my worries cutting me. If I go through with the initiation, Delilah won't want to know me.

'I hope Delilah don't take too long at the dentist, Miss,' I say. 'School will be boring without her.' I think about how upset she was when she saw the photograph this morning. 'It's awful for her, I think, when she misses her dad,' I say as I put the bags down.

'Well, having a good friend like you must really help,' says Miss Raquel.

'Do you think so, Miss?' I say.

'Yes, Marcus, I do. Friendship is everything,' says Miss Raquel.

And she's right. Friendship is everything and I can't lose Delilah.

School is nothing without Delilah by my side. I waited and waited for her to get back from the dentist, but my hope was crushed when Miss Raquel stopped me in the corridor to tell me that Florence had phoned the school and she was keeping Delilah at home for the rest of the day as she has a temperature and a sore throat.

She most probably caught a chill from being out all night on our Moon Dog adventure. Still, I bet Delilah thinks it was worth it. It's hard to believe I've only known her since last Friday.

There was a brief moment of happiness when Wilbur and Marnie came in and I was allowed to sit with Wilbur for a while, but most of the day was spent hiding from the Cinder Street Boyz. Everywhere I went, the three shadows of Sol, Nico and Baz followed me. They followed me into the toilet and were kicking at my door, kick, kick, kick. I was shaking, leaning against the door to stop them forcing it open until the caretaker turfed them out. I hid in the toilet till the bell rang and then went to the science lab, but there they were again, blocking the doorway, grinning at me. They must have checked my timetable. Thankfully, Mr Lawson shouted at them to get to their own lesson so I managed to duck into chemistry, avoiding their jibes, but as they walked away Nico shouted, 'We'll see you after school, Big M!'

Now, as the seconds march towards the end of the day, my worries start to strangle me. All

I can think about is that I don't want to be in the Cinder Street Boyz. Not now that I have Delilah in my life and Moon Dog too (sort of).

It's the last class of the day. I listen hard to the history teacher's words – anything to distract me from what's going to happen after school. We are learning about the Second World War and rationing. How during the war, everyone had to make the most use of what they'd got, and not waste things. So I decide to make the most of what I've got, and not waste paper. I relabel my exercise book.

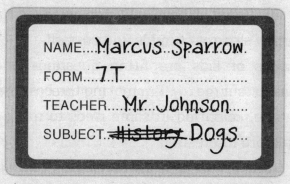

NAME...**Marcus Sparrow**.

FORM....**7T**...............

TEACHER....**Mr Johnson**.....

SUBJECT...~~History~~ **Dogs**...

I then delve to the bottom of my school bag for the dog lists I made in detention. I smooth the creases out on my lap and tuck my list in my new dog book.

I am half listening to Mr Johnson groaning on about how everyone had to grow their own vegetables, thinking that Nana Sparrow would've loved it.

I start to draw a map of the heath, dreaming of the places I could explore with Moon Dog, if only he were mine.

At the front of the class, Mr Johnson has stuck up a war-time poster of a large carrot wearing glasses, carrying a top hat and a briefcase. It says, *Doctor Carrot, the Children's best friend*. I shudder. This is a lie: carrots are my enemy, not my friend. I have still not got over Nana Sparrow's carrot crumble and custard.

Loads of kids are firing questions at Mr Johnson, but me . . . I'm making the best use of my time, colouring in some trees to make my map more interesting.

Just as I start to draw Moon Dog rolling on the grass to have his tummy tickled, the book is ripped from my lap under the desk by Mr Johnson. He has the face of thunder.

Mr Johnson starts waving my book in the

air and shouting, 'What is this? MARCUS SPARROW, HOW DARE YOU DEFACE SCHOOL PROPERTY!'

'I'm not, Sir.' I think fast. 'It's like what you said they did in the Second World War, not wasting paper. I am using one book for two purposes. It's my dog book and also my history book.' But I don't think Sir is buying my argument. 'Oh my goodness! I'm only doing like what Winston Churchill told us to. It's bad to waste paper. Nana Sparrow says, *waste not, want not*.'

Mr Johnson gives me the stare of death for the longest time, and then his lip starts to quiver, and he throws back his head and roars with laughter.

'Marcus Sparrow, you have an answer for everything, don't you?'

'I try to, Sir,' I say. But to be honest, I wasn't sure if it was one of those questions that you're not meant to answer.

'Get on with your work, all of you. I want you to write a story, pretending you are a child in the Second World War. Describe what you are having for tea.'

'Yes, Sir,' I say. 'That's easy. It's like that in our house every day.'

I am well into my story about a boy called Richard, who is being forced by his nana to eat carrots for breakfast, but the clock is ticking, and it's getting nearer and nearer to three thirty.

When the end-of-school bell rings, kids start pouring out of their lessons and racing across the playground to escape. Out of the window I see Nico, Sol and Baz at the gates. Waiting for me.

Desperate action is called for.

I need to do something big. Something that will get me into trouble.

As we begin to file out of the classroom, inspiration strikes.

I pick up my chair . . . and throw it at the window.

The glass cracks.

There is an echoing silence. The kids in my

class just gape at me. And as I look around at their faces I know for certain that if they weren't scared of me before, then I've done it now. My class will never want to know me.

'Marcus Sparrow,' hisses Mr Johnson. 'I suppose you have some clever answer ready for this dangerous behaviour.'

'No, Mr Johnson, it was me. I picked up the chair and I threw it.'

'Marcus Sparrow, head teacher's office. NOW.'

BINGO.

Mr Lawson shouts at me for about half an hour, telling me how serious this is and they are going to phone up Nana, but all I care about is the fact that I can see out of the window that the Cinder Street Boyz have gone And 'cause it's half term I won't have to see them for days.

I am going to be in for it when I get home.

So when I finally get dismissed and walk out of the school gates, I turn on my heel and head towards the Beckham Estate.

12

Delilah

I am not sick, not in the slightest. I hear Mum blatantly lying on the phone to Miss Raquel.

'Yes, she has a temperature and a sore throat. I know . . . I know, there's a lot of it going around . . .'

The truth is, Mum and I need to talk and we don't know how to. I have changed into my *101 Dalmatians* onesie and hidden from the world under my quilt. I am curled up into a cringing ball.

Memories of the visit to my new dentist flash through my brain.

I was lying in that enormous chair with my mouth wide open, and poor Mr Andrews was trying his very best to examine my teeth. But Mum was hovering. 'Be careful, Mr Andrews, her mouth is very delicate.'

Then she grabbed my hand. 'Be brave, darling, be brave.'

'Mrs Jones, sit down please,' said Mr Andrews. 'I am only polishing Delilah's teeth. Let me do my job – you are making your daughter so tense, she can't open her mouth properly.'

I hadn't realised that I was clenching my jaw, until he said it.

I whispered, 'Thank you,' to Mr Andrews before I attempted to open my mouth again.

He had to tell Mum to sit down three more times. It was mortifying!

Afterwards, we ordered a cab home from Lady Cabs, which is the only company Mum trusts if I need to go anywhere. We had our usual driver, Moira. I couldn't bring myself to even look at Mum, I couldn't trust myself to even speak. Mum just sat in the car, twiddling her bracelet. Moira kept looking at us through her mirror as we sat silently all the way home. It's a wonder she could even drive with all that crackling tension in the car.

Now I am cleaned, polished and fuming.

I have had enough. Mum is slowly, slowly

suffocating me. Today she has been a total nightmare!

There's a knock on my bedroom door and without waiting for my reply, Mum comes in carrying a tray with two bowls of Nana Sparrow's heated-up cauliflower cheese. She hands me a plate, perches on the edge of my bed and we start to eat. Still no words are said, but I notice her glance at the photo of me and Dad that Rosemary gave her. I have put it up on my bedside table.

I think I'm going to have to be the grown up and start this conversation. The conversation that has to be had.

'Mum, do you know, my earliest memory is on the beach? I don't know where it was. Me sitting on Dad's shoulders, gripping on really tight, and he was holding your hand, and you had on this green skirt, and it was billowing in the breeze, and we were laughing and you and Dad were splashing through the shallow waves, and we were all so free.'

'It was Margate,' says Mum, 'and you were about three. Your dad just woke up one morning and said, "Come, the sun is shining".'

'He would say that every half term,' I say, 'and in

134

the long school holidays. Trips to St Paul's Cathedral and up, up, up to the whispering gallery where Dad whispered into the wall that he loved me to the sun and back. And we took a ride on the London Eye, chewing toffees, and we went to the Tower of London to see the ravens, and saw the dinosaurs in the Natural History Museum. I cried because I thought they might be lonely and Dad had to explain that I couldn't have a pet dinosaur and I had to leave them in the museum for all the other boys and girls.'

Mum has tears splashing down her cheeks. 'I miss him so much,' she says.

I pile our nearly empty plates on top of each other, and shove them on the tray, cutching up to Mum so I can hold her close.

'So do I,' I say, 'but remember what he used to say?'

'Explore, be free,' says Mum.

'Exactly. What would he think of you gripping on to me and not letting me grow? I need to breathe, Mum.'

And now I can't stop the tears and as I sit cheek to cheek with Mum my tears flow into hers and we make one river.

'I am scared I am going to lose you too,' says Mum.

'Mum, you won't lose me. Please let me grow up. Trust me, stop checking up on me all the time.'

'I'll try, I promise I'll try,' says Mum.

'How about this puppy you promised me?' I say, laughing and wiping my face on my onesie sleeve.

'A puppy will be a good start to our new life,' says Mum. 'We can go on lovely walks together.'

'Yes we can,' I say. 'I promise we will, but you've got to let me go on walks with Marcus and by myself too.'

'It's a deal, Delilah Jones,' she says. 'But you've got to promise me that you will always take your phone and let me know what time you'll be back.'

'It's a deal.' And Mum and I shake hands on this new part of our life without my dad. I miss him.

I switch on my laptop and the puppy adverts that I look at all the time ping back up on the screen. The photo of the pug puppies sitting in an armchair, in front of the pink wallpaper. Mum nuzzles up next to me, her arm around my shoulder.

'Look, Mum, so sweet. Oh! Look at those Cavalier pups, snuggling on that white sheepskin rug.

They're adorable. Look, it says "call Ivan". Let's just call him for a chat about the puppies, tell him we are interested. Oh, Mum, look at the little dachshunds.'

'A lot of people call dachshunds sausage dogs,' says Mum. 'When I was a little girl, my next-door neighbour Edie had a little black one. Bertie, he was called.'

'Bertie the sausage dog,' I say, laughing, 'that's a brilliant name.'

I click on to another photo. 'Oh, Mum, these dachshunds are just so cute, five little sausage dogs all sitting in a row on the sofa. Mum, we need to phone the numbers on these adverts, say we are interested before they all go.'

'Delilah, calm down,' says Mum, 'these puppies are a lot of money and I'll have to find it from somewhere before we can even start calling anyone.'

'Oh, please, Mum, please. I'll do all my homework without a fuss, I promise.'

But before she can say anything more, the doorbell rings.

13

Marcus

I feel like I, Marcus Sparrow, have walked in on the most private of all moments and I shouldn't be here. I can see that Delilah and Florence have both been crying.

My words fall out of my mouth on top of each other.

'Delilah, sorry you're sick. I got you sweets for your sore throat and this magazine, *Planet Dog*, to read, here you go.' And I shove all the things I bought for Delilah with my pocket money from the newsagent's into her hand.

'I'll leave you two to it,' says Florence and she goes out of the room.

Delilah leans forwards and grabs my arm.

'Quick,' she hisses, 'Moon Dog, was he there

this morning?'

'No,' I say. 'No sign of Leopard Tattoo and Nose Ring either.'

I hear the landline ring and Florence answer it.

'They've gone again,' I continue. 'I just don't understand what's happening next door.'

The sound of the receiver being replaced and footsteps.

Delilah coughs dramatically and throws herself back on her pillow.

'You faker, Delilah, you've skived school.'

'Sometimes, Marcus, the mind needs to rest too,' says Delilah, and I see her chin quivering and look into her brown eyes and I can tell she's hurting, and she has had enough of being sad and that her *had enough* is rising up through her.

Before I can think of anything to say, Florence comes back into the room with two glasses of orange juice with bits in.

'Marcus, that was your nana on the phone. She wanted to check if you were here. She doesn't sound very happy, and said you are to go home at once. Drink this first, there's a wind sprung up outside. Get a bit of vitamin C down you.'

'Thank you very much, Florence,' I say, my heart plummeting at the thought of facing Nana Sparrow.

'Naughty, naughty. What have you done, Marcus?' says Delilah, twinkling at me.

'Ah nothing,' I lie, 'the teachers just moaning on as usual. But I got one of my feelings that I'm going to be grounded over half term, so it's good I'm seeing you now, just in case my premonition comes true.'

Florence laughs and kisses me on the cheek.

'You are a kind boy, Marcus, and thanks for being a good friend to my Delilah.'

'You're embarrassing him, Mum!' says Delilah.

I feel my cheeks burning and I down my orange juice in one and leave to face the Nana Sparrow music.

As I walk across the courtyard of the Beckham Estate, thinking Moon Dog thoughts as I go, I feel my feet walking towards the wasteland, away from the direction of the bus stop. *It's healthier to walk*, I reason with myself, but I know the truth is that it will take longer. My walk slows to a trudge and my trudge to pigeon steps, daring myself to take as long as possible to get home. The wind is in my face and my bones are heavy and there in front of me is the Beckham Animal Rescue Centre.

A red car drives over the bumpy grass, and toots its horn as it passes me. Marnie is at the wheel, and Wilbur is sitting in the back of the car, his nose pressed against the window. My pigeon steps turn to running in a blink of a second.

Marnie gets out of her car and the wind is now so strong that she staggers backwards a few steps. Wilbur is barking his hellos to me.

'Hi, Marcus,' she says.

'Do you work here, Marnie?' I say.

'Yes I do. When I am not taking Wilbur into schools, I help out at the rescue centre. Would you mind getting Wilbur out of the car and holding on to his lead? I've got some boxes of posters and flyers to take into the centre.'

'Of course,' I say, feeling, as Nana says, like all my Christmases have come at once.

'Hello, Wilbur,' I say as I let him out of the car. I hold his lead tight and drop to my knees to give him a hug. He gives me a Staffie kiss.

I follow Marnie into the reception of the Beckham Animal Rescue Centre.

We start to unpack the flyers that say *#AdoptDontShop* and have a picture of a cute scruffy mongrel called Bob with the words **Can You Give A Rescue Dog A Forever Home?**

Matt the Vet walks into the reception.

'Marcus Sparrow, what are you doing here?'

'I am being helpful, Matt,' I say.

'Well,' he chuckles, 'I think helpful deserves a reward. Would you like to see some puppies?'

'Yes. Yes. Yes pleeeease,' I say.

'Follow me.'

He leads me through a room to the left of reception. I can hear barking and yelping from somewhere off to the right.

'It's dinner-time,' says Matt, 'so the dogs, as you can hear, are very excited.'

We walk down a corridor to a room at the end, and as soon as I walk in, I feel this peaceful mood.

In the corner is a whelping box, and inside a beautiful golden retriever and five of the most gorgeous squidgy puppies. I can hardly breathe. They are tumbling over each other, exploring their world and yelping and play biting. The mother dog is gently nuzzling and licking her puppies.

'A kind man who lives round the corner found the mother abandoned in Kensington Gardens – she was stretched out next to the Peter Pan statue, just staring up at the sky for hours as if she was waiting for something. We've called her Sky,' says Matt. 'We think the father is a German shepherd dog. These pups already have loving families to adopt them, once they are old enough to leave their mother.'

'Those families are just so lucky,' I say, wishing with every bone in my body that I could have a dog, and that Moon Dog were mine.

A woman in jeans and a purple Beckham

Animal Rescue T-shirt is kneeling by the box. Her nametag says 'Jessica'. She carefully picks up a brown puppy with a black patch over his eye.

'The rest of them we called after characters in *Peter Pan*,' says Jessica. 'The little black one is Wendy, the little golden one running around looking for mischief is Tinker Bell, the other golden one who's falling asleep is Tiger Lily, the little black and brown one is Peter Pan and this little one,' she says, holding the puppy for me to take, 'is Smee.'

Smee snuggles into my shoulder, making little whimpering sounds. I sniff his warm puppy smell, and he licks me with his tiny tongue. The Cinder Street Boyz and broken windows and Dad's sadness cloud all disappear because there is only room in these puppy-filled seconds for happiness. But then the broken-window thoughts seep back. There was zero chance before of me getting a dog; now that I'm in trouble, it's minus a thousand zeros.

Jessica is watching me.

'You have a lovely gentle way about you, um . . . ?'

'I'm Marcus,' I say, thinking how no one has ever called me gentle in my life, but when I'm here with the puppies, all my angry thoughts float away. Just like when I'm with Delilah.

'Marcus,' she says. 'I can tell how much you love dogs.'

'I do, more than anything in the whole wide world,' I say.

And now that I feel better, I know it's time to face Nana Sparrow. I give little Smee a kiss and pat the mother dog.

'Thank you so much, Sky,' I say to the golden retriever, 'for letting me meet your puppies. Goodbye everyone and thank you.' I start the walk home dreaming of my Moon Dog and puppies called Smee.

When I get there, Nana Sparrow is standing in the open doorway waiting for me. And what's scary is that she doesn't even shout.

She says very quietly, 'Get inside now.'

14

Marcus

'You threw a chair through a window?' says Nana Sparrow.

The disappointment in her eyes cuts me deep. But I can't tell her why I did it. I just can't. So I stand there and take my punishment.

'Sometimes I don't understand your behaviour at all.' She shakes her head.

'Sorry, Nana Sparrow,' I say.

'You will not see Delilah for the whole of half term.'

My heart drops to my knees.

'You are grounded in the evenings, but as for the daytime, well, I have come to an agreement with your school,' she says. 'Over half term you will work for me on my market stall and your wages will pay for the window to be replaced.'

'Yes, Nana,' I say, my heart dropping to my trainers. It's going to be a long half term.

The next day, she drags me out of bed early and sets me to work.

I try and explain to her that this is child labour, and against the laws of this country, but she's not having it.

'Potatoes,' I mutter, 'come get your potatoes.'

Nana Sparrow pokes me in the chest with her finger, hard.

'SPUDS!' I yell. 'COME AND GET YOUR SPUDS, TWO BAGS FOR THE PRICE OF ONE.'

Nana doesn't let me out of her beady sight, not once, but to be honest I'm relieved, 'cause I am sure I just spied Baz, Sol and Nico, lurking like a bad smell, watching me, from between the jewellery and vintage furniture stalls. I look again and they've gone, but if it was them, they can't get to me, not with Nana Sparrow around.

Wednesday chugs by really slowly. At the end of the day, I can't wait to get home to see if there is any sign of Moon Dog but the FOR SALE sign is stuck firmly in the ground, and the house stands deserted and silent.

Dad is still in bed. He doesn't get up once. Not even just to say hello.

On Thursday, Mr Lawson comes to Nana's stall to buy some fruit and veg and I just want the ground to swallow me up.

'Ah, good, good,' he says. 'Taking your punishment, I see.'

I can feel my cheeks burning up as Nana Sparrow bags his potatoes and gives him a discount.

'I've got him working hard, don't you worry, Mr Lawson.'

And she has. I am running backwards and forwards, fetching and carrying for the rest of the day.

By Friday evening, my bones are aching with tiredness but my longing to see Moon Dog aches even more.

Nana has parked the van outside our house. She marches down the path and unlocks our front door.

'Bring that box of parsnips in, Marcus,' she calls over her shoulder.

'Yes, Nana Sparrow,' I shout, reaching into the back of the van. I grab the box and I step on the pavement, straight into Leopard Tattoo.

'Oy, watch where you're going.'

'Sorry,' I say. 'Really sorry.' Then, like Nana always taught me to say, 'I beg your pardon.'

'It's all right, no harm done,' he growls.

I race down our path with the heavy box and put it just inside our front door, and bend and pretend to do up my trainer lace, so I can watch where Leopard Tattoo is going.

With a screech of brakes, a blue car pulls up, driven by Nose Ring. Leopard Tattoo jumps in, slams the door, the engine revs, and the car pulls away.

Grabbing the box of parsnips, I kick our front door shut and run down our hall into the kitchen. I hear Nana Sparrow upstairs shouting at Dad to get out of bed.

I unbolt the back door and race into the back garden. I look over the fence. Next door's garden is empty. No Moon Dog.

I look up at the house and my heart backflips. My Moon Dog is looking out of the kitchen window. He must be standing on his back legs and resting on the sink.

The key! I think.

I feel under the top crate and grab next door's key.

'Hello, boy,' I call, as I clamber over the fence and run up to the back door. Moon Dog is barking.

Holding my breath, I turn the key in the lock. It opens and I step inside, praying that the men don't come back and catch me breaking in. I shut the door behind me, dropping the key back safely in my pocket. Moon Dog is so excited to see me – he jumps up, nearly knocking me over, as he puts his paws round my neck, like he is giving me a cuddle. I hug the dog-bear back.

'Down, Moon Dog, good boy.' He picks up the rubber bone toy I brought him and brings it to me.

'Thank you, Moon Dog,' I say, taking the

slobbery toy from his mouth.

But I haven't got time to play fetch; I need to take this chance to look for more clues and work out what is going on in this house. The men could be back at any second!

On the kitchen counter, next to the cooker, is the large cardboard box filled with mobile phones – each one now has a sticker on it.

I take a phone out. 'Dachshund – George' is written on it in scrawny writing. I pick up another and turn it over. 'Pug – Barry' the sticker says on this one. I check them all. 'Toy poodle – Graham', 'French bulldog – Alvin', 'Cavalier – Ivan', and so on. All the phones have stickers on them with different dog breeds and names.

It doesn't make sense.

I walk into the front room, followed by Moon Dog. Everything is as it was before – the yellow sofa is in the middle of the room and the big wooden chest is by the window and the shutters are still shut. I stand on my tiptoes and peep into the chest. Moon Dog stands on his hind legs next to me and does the same, wagging his tail.

Inside the chest are all the things that were there before, one of those tall lamps on a stand and lots of cushions, a stripy rug, mugs, a kettle and a coffee machine. There is also a huge purple velvet curtain and a shopping bag holding those loaves of bread that come half-baked, which you shove in the oven to finish them off. Nana gets us those sometimes for a treat. My tummy rumbles. I'm suddenly very hungry.

'What are these for, eh, Moon Dog? What are your owners up to?'

Moon Dog runs out of the room, into the hall and up the stairs. He stops half way and barks, like he wants me to follow, so I sprint up the stairs after him.

Moon Dog bounds into a big back bedroom where a camera is set up on a tripod. The walls are decorated with sections of different wallpapers that don't go together. On one side there's this pink paper, with an armchair in front of it. Next to that is a wide strip of that posh paper with a velvety flower pattern, what you get in stately homes. Then there's a section of stripy wallpaper which really clashes next to the flock. On the floor is a pile of different coloured rugs. I pull up a sheepskin rug and put it in front of the pink wall, and look through the camera.

Through the lens, it looks like we are in a completely different room. I play about with the camera and depending on what section of the wall the camera is pointed at, you can believe that you are in lots of separate houses. Why? Why would anybody do that?

Moon Dog barks. I hear a car pull up outside, and a door slam. I tear down the stairs. The sound of a key in the lock. Moon Dog growls. No time to escape. I dive into the front room, behind the wooden chest, and curl up in a ball, just in time.

Moon Dog doesn't come near me, as if he knows that I shouldn't be there. Clever dog! Instead, he bounds around the room like a lunatic, his claws clattering on the bare floorboards.

I hear footsteps as the men come into the front room.

I shut my eyes, cross my fingers and make a wish that they don't look behind the chest.

'Dratted dog! How did you get out of the kitchen?'

'We'd better get moving, Frank, we've not got a lot of time.'

'George, you've gotta call me George. She wants a dachshund.'

'OK, well get on with it, George! Bread in the oven. Put some coffee on as well, to add to the nice family home smell. Always does the trick. It's just like selling a house. Put the mugs out, while you're at it – she might want a cuppa. Oh, and put some toilet roll in the loo. Did you find that missing key?'

My heart literally stops.

'No. I reckon I must've put it in my pocket without thinking and it's dropped out somewhere, good thing we've got spares.'

My heart starts beating again. Fast.

What would they do to me if they found out I had taken the key – or discover that I am hiding in this very room listening to every word they are saying?

I hold my breath as they start taking the lamp, the stripy rug and other things out of the wooden chest.

The edge of the purple velvet curtain comes fluttering down on me, as it is thrown over the chest.

'There you go, George – now it looks like a table.'

Why is someone coming to get a dachshund from Nose Ring and Leopard Tattoo?

The corner of the curtain is tickling my nose. I screw my face up, so that I don't sneeze.

'Right, let's make this room look lived in. Make yourself useful, Dog. Come here, let me rub these cushions on you. Stand still,' I hear Nose Ring say.

Moon Dog barks.

'Shut up, Dog.'

I curl my fists up tight. I hate the way they talk to Moon Dog. To them, he is just a dog with no name.

Cramp sears through my calf. I bite my lip to stop myself from crying out.

'Right, that should do it,' he says, 'cushions covered in hair, like the dog lives here.'

I hear the two men leave. I leap up and rub the back of my leg like crazy.

Moon Dog thinks it's a game and jumps up and licks my nose. I can see through the slats of the window shutters that the FOR SALE sign is not there.

Footsteps.

I flick back the corner of the purple velvet curtain, and climb inside the chest, pulling the material back over the corner just in time.

There is a small gap between the slats of wood that I can peep through. I see Moon Dog scampering around.

The men walk back in. Leopard Tattoo is carrying a cage, crammed full of the tiniest little yelping dachshund puppies. He dumps the cage on the floor and opens it, but the puppies have wide frightened eyes and are shrinking away from the open door of the cage. They don't want to come out and explore like Peter Pan, Tinker Bell, Wendy, Tiger Lily and Smee did. I bite my lip hard to stop myself from reaching out to them. *It's all right, little ones, don't be scared. Marcus is here.*

'Come on, you little money-makers,' Nose Ring says as he scoops the puppies out of the cage one by one. 'Be cute, win the heart of the lady.'

I count six of them – four are black and tan and two are cream-coloured. They are all smooth-haired.

The puppies scurry around on the floorboards as if they have landed on a strange planet. One does a wee on the floor and three of them hide behind the sofa. But where's the rough and tumble and play-biting like Smee and his brothers and sisters did as they explored their world? The little things seem so very scared of everything around them. It's like they've never been in a house before.

Where have they come from? I wonder.

Leopard Tattoo leaves the room and then I hear barking from the hallway. He comes back in carrying a fully grown black-and-tan dachshund,

'There you go, you play mother,' says Leopard Tattoo, placing the dog in the middle of the floor.

What does he mean, *play mother*? I don't understand.

Nose Ring scoops the puppies from behind the sofa and puts them next to the mother dog – but she totally ignores them, which is so odd. No licking, no nuzzling . . . nothing. Is that why Leopard Tattoo said *play mother*? Like the dog is an actor playing a part? She obviously isn't the puppies' mother. This is terrible!

Moon Dog is running around licking the tiny dogs, trying to make friends, but the puppies quiver. I don't think they know what friends are. This is the saddest thing I've ever seen!

A yummy smell of bread wafts into the room.

Please, please, tummy, don't gurgle with hunger. Not now!

The doorbell rings.

'Hello, I've come to see George about a dachshund.'

I know that voice.

'Yes, I'm George. Do come in. Welcome, welcome.'

Peeping through the hole, I spy Florence, Delilah's mum. She steps into the room, carrying a puppy carrier. It's sky blue, Delilah's favourite colour.

'Gosh, he's enormous,' says Florence, patting Moon Dog on the head. Moon Dog rolls over to have his tummy tickled.

'We are dog mad in this house,' says Leopard Tattoo.

Nose Ring and Leopard Tattoo are also making an actor out of Moon Dog, pretending he is their much-loved family pet.

Then Florence sees the puppies.

'Ah,' she says, 'they are gorgeous. Do you mind if I sit down?'

'No, please do, where are my manners? Whoops, sorry, let me brush the dog hair off the cushion,' says Leopard Tattoo. 'We live for dogs in this house, as you can see. We'll be sad to see the puppies go, we've grown very attached.'

What lies! The puppies have never been here before – it's so obvious. As I look through the gap in the chest, I can see they are still not acting like puppies should. They are not exploring the room, or wagging their tails and getting up to mischief like Peter Pan, Wendy, Tiger Lily, Tinker Bell and Smee. Can't Florence see that they are cowering as they look around the room with their scared eyes? The tiniest of all, a beautiful little cream sausage dog, walks up to the chest where I am hiding, sniffs, and then curls up and goes to sleep. My arms ache to pick up the tiny pup and show him what love is.

Nose Ring carries in a tray of steaming mugs of coffee and a plate of biscuits. 'There you are, Mrs Jones. Make yourself at home.'

It's not their home, they don't even live here!

It's Mr Anderson's house.

I want Florence to ask these men lots of questions, to be suspicious. But I see Florence just take a sip of coffee as she looks around her contently.

'I lost my husband in a traffic accident,' she says.

'I am so sorry for your loss,' says Leopard Tattoo.

'Thank you,' says Florence. 'It's why I'm here. My daughter Delilah has had to be so very brave and I want this to be a lovely surprise. She has been begging for a puppy for months.'

Oh, no! I don't want Delilah to have a puppy from these men. I watch Florence take another sip of coffee and look at the little puppies. Why can't she see that something is wrong here?

'Some people call them sausage dogs,' says Florence.

'Yes, that's right,' says Nose Ring.

'They are very well-behaved.' The pretend-mother dachshund scrambles on to the sofa, next to Florence, and she pats her on the head.

'I read that you should always see the puppies with their mother.'

'That's right,' says Leopard Tattoo. 'Angel is a much-loved family pet. We call her Angel 'cause she is one. She is very placid and her puppies have her temperament.'

Florence walks towards my hiding place and bends down to look at the little cream sausage dog. The flowery yellow material of her dress covers the gap I am peeping through.

'I think I'll take this one.'

'Oh, he's a lovely little boy. You won't be sorry.'

'He seems so quiet and well-behaved. I think he will be a good companion for my daughter. A calm puppy will be a good influence on her, because my daughter is definitely not quiet and well-behaved.'

They all laugh.

I want to scream, NO, PUPPIES SHOULDN'T BE THAT QUIET! PUPPIES ARE NOT MEANT TO BE CALM AND WELL-BEHAVED!

Half of me wants to jump out of the chest and stop her buying the puppy, but I might end up in Young Offenders, like Sol's brother, for breaking and entering, and then I'll be no help to Delilah, or Moon Dog, and Nana Sparrow will most probably kill me, and then I'll be dead, and no use to anyone.

'So, I owe you one thousand, yes?' And I see Florence counting out all that money into George's – or whatever his name is – hand. A big wad of cash.

'I'm sorry it's some days since our phone call. It took me a while to get the money together,' says Florence. 'I sold a bracelet and a couple of rings my late husband bought me. It was hard to let them go but I know he would have wanted Delilah to have the puppy.'

'No worries. You are here now, and it'll be worth every penny. He's a much-loved puppy, from a much-loved family pet, from a good family home,' says Nose Ring, handing Florence a folder. 'All the paperwork you need for the little fellow is in there.'

I have to dig my nails into the palms of my hand, to stop myself crying out, LIARS, LIARS, LIARS.

He lifts the little cream sausage dog into Florence's dog carrier.

'This is going to be the best surprise ever for my daughter.'

The two men walk her out of the room, and to the front door.

I hear them talking on the doorstep, so I take my chance and clamber out of the chest.

Moon Dog jumps up and licks my nose.

'See you soon, Moon Dog.' I give him a quick pat on the head before I run out of the room. The front door is open, and I can see the men talking to Florence at the gate. I run through the back door, and across the grass and clamber over the fence.

I've made it!

But my relief turns to uneasiness as I think about what I have just witnessed. Everything about this is wrong.

I hide the key under my top crate and then I

climb up to sit in my thinking place, waggling my hand round and round in the hole, thinking my thoughts and piecing together the puzzle.

A bell rings in my brain as I think of the strange room with all the different coloured wallpapers and rugs.

The puppy advert we looked at on Delilah's laptop!

The pugs in that photo were sitting on the armchair, in front of pink wallpaper. The Cavalier pups were on the sheepskin rug, and the French bulldog puppies were playing on a yellow rug against the stripy wallpaper. They were all taken in that very room next door. The six dachshund puppies in the advert were sitting on that very yellow sofa. The mobiles with the breeds and the different men's names! It's totally fake! It's all Leopard Tattoo and Nose Ring. They are pretending to be lots of different people, who live in different houses, and it's all here, in Mr Anderson's old house, that's meant to be empty! The words I heard whispered in the night, the first time I saw Moon Dog –

French . . . paperwork. They weren't talking about going on holiday to France at all. I bet they were talking about paperwork for a French bulldog.

I remember what Matt the Vet told us, in his talk at school – that a reputable breeder will only ever have one breed. Nose Ring and Leopard Tattoo are most definitely not reputable breeders. They are con men and liars.

My thoughts wander back over the short time since I have known Delilah.

The lady in the red dress carrying a box out of next door the day Delilah came to tea. I bet there was a puppy in the box. A flashback to the box in Leopard Tattoo's car boot, that time Delilah and I were hiding behind a tree, watching him come out of Grayson & Stoat. I bet there was a puppy inside that box as well.

And Florence has just bought a puppy for Delilah from these lying, cheating men. And now I don't know what to do. I can't tell Nana Sparrow – she will kill me for going next door. If only I could ask Dad what to do.

Our back door swings open. Delilah is running down the garden towards me.

'Surprise!' she says.

'Delilah, what are you doing here?' I say, jumping off my thinking crates.

'Well, Marcus Sparrow, it seems that you have been behaving,' she says, looking at me through her eyelashes, like she does. 'Your nana says to tell you that you are no longer grounded.'

'Have you seen your mum?' I ask, my heart thudding, knowing full well that she hasn't and that when Delilah does, she is going to get what she wants most in the whole world.

I cross my fingers behind my back and make a silent wish, *Please, please may Delilah and her new puppy be really happy together.*

'No, she's been out ages as it happens,' says Delilah. 'She just phoned, said she was at the market, but it sounded more like she was in a car, if you ask me. She was acting all weird, said I was to hop into the cab she had ordered for me to come and invite you all to supper and that I was to look sharp. Ta-da!' she says, waving her arms in the air.

Then she whispers, 'Have you seen Moon Dog?'

'Yes,' I say. 'I . . .' But I can't tell her what I've just seen. I can't spoil that she is about to get a puppy, the thing she wants most on the whole planet.

So instead I say, 'Moon Dog was so pleased to see me. I gave him a hug from you, Delilah.'

She smiles and I am saved from Delilah's questions by Nana Sparrow shouting down the garden, 'HURRY UP, YOU TWO. FLORENCE IS WAITING FOR US. SHE JUST CALLED AND SAYS IT'S FISH AND CHIPS FOR SUPPER, AND I FOR ONE AM STARVING.'

Delilah cracks up laughing and I hold my hand up to give my friend, who I have missed so much, a high-five.

15

Delilah

I give Marcus a high-five. I've missed him so much. He is grinning at me from ear to ear but he has anxious eyes.

Nana Sparrow is waiting for us by the front door in her coat.

'Come on, you two,' she says, grabbing a scarf.

'Nana Sparrow, it's not even cold outside,' I say.

'Oh, you never know,' she says, winking at me.

'Would your dad like to come, Marcus? Mum wants to thank you all for the help you gave us with our flat.'

Marcus and Nana Sparrow exchange glances.

'Dad don't like fish and chips,' says Marcus, rather too quickly.

But I know it's really 'cause his dad is upstairs in

bed with the sadness.

We pile into the front of the Sparrow's Fruit & Veg van.

'Mum's been letting me have a bit more freedom,' I say as we drive down the road. 'I can tell she finds it hard, but she has been letting me go on little walks by myself over half term.'

'That's big progress,' says Nana. 'You have both had your planet shaken and it will take time to rebuild your world. Be patient with her, Delilah.'

'I will, Nana Sparrow. I promise. Marcus, it wasn't the same without you, walking along, swinging my dog lead singing our song. It just wasn't the same.'

We start to sing our song.

'We are le le le lead walking
Though we ain't got a dog
Lead walking through the park and the bog
We are lead walking
We are telling no lies
Lead walking the dogs in disguise . . .'

We sing it over and over, all the way to the Beckham Estate.

And all the way in the lift up to the fourth floor.

As I ring on the bell, Nana Sparrow blindfolds me with her scarf. I literally can't see a thing.

'What's happening?' I cry out into the dark. Mum takes my hand, and I can feel we are going in the direction of the front room. She guides me to the sofa and sits me down.

'Right,' she says, 'sit very still.'

I feel something small and warm in my lap. I rip my blindfold off, and there is MY PUPPY. MY VERY OWN SAUSAGE DOG PUPPY. The tiniest, creamiest dachshund I have ever seen, looking up at me. And I fill up with love, more love than I thought it was ever possible to experience. I feel as if my whole life has been leading up to this very point.

'Oh, Mum,' I whisper. 'Thank you.' Tears are splashing down my cheeks, and I don't care, I'm just so happy. 'Thank you, Mum, oh, thank you.'

As Mum wipes my cheeks with a tissue, I see that her wrist and fingers are bare.

'Mum, your jewellery?'

She quickly pulls her sleeve over her hand.

'Mum?'

'It's OK. They went to the puppy fund.'

'But Dad bought you those . . .'

'He would have wanted you to have the puppy.'

'I . . . I don't know what to say.'

She kisses the top of my head.

My puppy licks my hand with his tiny tongue and looks up at me, and my heart falls into his wide brown eyes. As I stroke my little boy I look around the room at everyone drinking in my joy. Mum is laughing and crying at the same time. Nana Sparrow is smiling down at me and I can see her eyes are watering. And Marcus . . . Why isn't Marcus smiling?

'What are you going to call your doggy?' says Nana Sparrow.

I glimpse our table, all set for our lovely fish and chip supper, and the perfect name comes to me in an arrow of inspiration.

'Well, I think as our "thank you to the Sparrows" fish and chip supper is also our "welcome puppy to our family" party, I should call my puppy Chip. And besides, he's a sausage dog and I love sausage and chips.'

Everyone laughs except Marcus, who is looking

down at the carpet, scuffing his foot. What is wrong with him?

Mum and Nana Sparrow go through to the kitchen, chatting.

'Chip is close to the ground when he walks, like me,' I say, trying to make Marcus laugh.

He doesn't laugh.

'Marcus, do you want to hold him? Chip, say hello to grumpy Marcus. What's the matter with you?' I hiss.

'Nothing,' he grunts as he plonks himself on the sofa next to me.

He could show more happiness for me.

Maybe Marcus is jealous? It just doesn't seem like him.

'I'll let you take turns when we walk him on Parliament Hill.'

'Thanks,' he says, and oh-so gently strokes Chip's ears, but his eyes still look so anxious.

'His ears are so warm,' he says.

Mum and Nana Sparrow bring through steaming plates of fish and chips. They smell delicious.

Mum produces two shiny new little bowls and a

plastic mat with little paw prints running across it.

'We've got to start as we mean to go on, Delilah. You need to leave Chip to eat in peace while you eat your own supper.'

I put Chip gently on the carpet.

I take the mat and bowls from Mum; one has water in it, the other food. I place the bowls on the mat.

'It's special puppy food,' says Mum. 'I did my research and this is a good brand, gives them all the nutrients they need.'

I turn to encourage Chip to walk to the bowls and have his supper but he is completely frozen to the spot.

'He doesn't like the feel of the carpet under his paws,' says Marcus.

I pick Chip up and cuddle him. As soon as his feet leave the carpet, I feel him relax. I stroke his ears and my tiny puppy snuggles into me.

Marcus is watching me from the doorway, chewing his lip.

'I think my little Chip just wants cuddles all the time,' I say.

'We should make Chip a little den, so he feels safe,' says Marcus.

I run to my bedroom to get my sky-blue comfort blanket and Marcus makes a little circle of cushions on the floor. I put the blanket inside the circle, in front of the plastic mat and bowls, so that Chip can be comfortable while he eats.

I lift Chip on to the blanket and he laps some water but turns his nose away from his food.

'He's standing funny,' says Marcus.

His head is hanging and his tail is just drooping like he's all kind of tucked in. But still I respond, 'No he's not, he's just a baby and he's still learning about standing.' I stamp on the pinprick of doubt that tickles my mind. *Please wag your little tail, Chip,* I think, *please, please, please. Show everyone you are happy in your new home.*

'Go on, Chip, eat your supper,' I say, but my little puppy is sick on the carpet.

Nana Sparrow gets some paper towels to clean it up. 'He's probably just a little over-excited being in a new home,' says Nana. 'Leave him to eat in his own good time.'

'Yes, that's it! He's just over-excited. I think you're right, Nana Sparrow.' I grip on to her words with all of my heart.

'Wash your hands and sit at the table, both of you,' says Nana Sparrow.

'I will in a minute,' says Marcus. 'I'm just watching Chip for now.'

'Now, Marcus,' says Nana Sparrow.

I stroke Chip one more time and then go to wash my hands. Marcus follows me in body but his thoughts are with the stars. He lets the soap slip and slide in his hands and the cold water slops over the side.

'Watch out!' I say, pulling the plug out. 'Please tell me what's wrong. This is meant to be a party.'

'Nothing,' he says, and leaves the bathroom.

As I dry my hands I vow I will not let him spoil this for me.

I join everyone at the table with a big smile.

'Let's celebrate,' I say and we all sit down and start tucking in to our celebration fish and chip supper.

'This really is most kind of you,' says Nana Sparrow. 'Isn't it, Marcus?'

'Humph,' grunts Marcus.

'We should make a toast on this special day,' I say, ignoring Marcus as I pour everyone a glass of Coke.

'To Chip and friendship,' I say.

'To Chip and friendship,' everyone repeats.

'I chose Chip, because he seemed such a quiet, well-behaved little puppy,' says Mum.

'Puppies are not meant to be quiet and well-behaved, they are meant to be lively and energetic, exploring the world and getting up to mischief. That's what puppies do,' mutters Marcus, stuffing chips in his mouth.

Marcus is seriously getting on my nerves now.

I was so happy for him when he told me about Moon Dog.

'Chip will explore the world when he is ready,' I say, shaking salt on my chips. 'He is just taking his time to get to know his new home. That's all.' And I take a big bite of fish, as I am starving.

'Oh, Marcus,' says Mum. 'I just wanted a good little puppy.'

'Bless him, the little fella's asleep,' says Nana Sparrow.

I look to see my baby Chip curled up by his water dish. He really is so very tiny and it's like a fire has lit inside me and I just want to protect him from the world. With every breath I take, I love him more and more.

Just then, a loud sound rumbles from the kitchen as the washing machine switches from the wash cycle to spin. Chip wakes up with a jump and starts yelping, pushing through the cushion wall of his den, and lands on the television remote, which had fallen off the sofa on to the floor. The TV flicks on, blasting a quiz programme into the room. Chip shakes like a jelly.

I leap out of my chair.

'I'm here, Chip. Delilah's here,' I say, scooping him up. But he is wriggling, like he's panicked.

Marcus grabs the remote and turns the television off. I sit on the sofa with Chip on my knee, stroking his ears till he calms.

Marcus sits next to me, putting his arm round my shoulder.

'You're doing well, Delilah. Chip knows already that he's safe with you. And he's only just met you, remember.'

'Chip feels the love I have for him,' I say, smiling up at Marcus, relieved he's stopped acting all moody.

'Goodness me,' says Nana Sparrow. 'Chip's scared of his own shadow; anyone would think he's not been in a house before.'

'Oh he has. Actually, it's a bit of a coincidence. Chip was born in the house next to yours in Mabel Street,' says Mum. 'They love dogs, don't they, your neighbours? I met their massive Newfoundland. Dog hair everywhere, there was.'

Cold creeps up from my feet. 'Moon Dog,' I blurt out before I can stop myself. Marcus digs me hard in the ribs with his elbow.

'The house next to ours?' repeats Nana Sparrow.

'Yes, I got Chip from your next-door neighbour, George, a lovely man he was. It was my little secret,' says Mum, smiling round at everyone.

'The house next door is empty, Florence, you must be mistaken. It's been empty for ages. They can't seem to sell it, for some reason,' says Nana Sparrow.

179

Marcus stands up so quickly, me and Chip jump. It's like he's got a rocket in his feet and he's pacing up and down, up and down, and then his words burst out of him like a letter explosion.

'Florence is not mistaken, she did buy Chip from next door. And I know 'cause I was there.'

The cold reaches my belly, and Mum is staring at Marcus, like she's seen a ghost.

'How, how were you there?' she asks.

'I broke into next door,' he says.

'YOU BROKE INTO NEXT DOOR?' explodes Nana Sparrow.

'I wanted to see what was going on,' says Marcus. 'The house is being used to sell puppies, Nana. There's a man with a leopard tattoo and a man with a nose ring, and they've got lots of phones with different numbers, and they pretend to be different people, but it's all them. They've been in and out of the house, and they've got a Newfoundland, and they don't even love him . . . but I love him and I've called him Moon Dog. I was in the house checking Moon Dog was OK and then the men came back, so I hid in the chest. I was there when you bought the puppy, Florence. That yellow dress you've got on is the same colour as their sofa, and you paid the man with a leopard tattoo on his arm one thousand pounds in cash.'

The cold reaches my heart. My kind Mum sold her precious jewellery from Dad and gave Leopard Tattoo and Nose Ring all of her money. Mum looks as if she's going to cry and at this precise moment I hate Marcus for doing this to her. I hate him.

My thoughts race; there must be some sort of simple explanation. My baby Chip is just so gorgeous. I hug my puppy close and stamp hard on my cold doubt.

'No, no, no, this can't be right,' splutters Mum. 'Maybe, they've just moved in and they just haven't introduced themselves to you yet? The puppies were probably born in their old house. Yes, that must be it. I did everything they tell you to. I saw the puppies with the mother dog and . . .'

'Yes,' says Marcus, 'and the dog was ignoring them.'

I feel sick as the cold rises to my throat.

'She probably wanted a rest,' says Mum, 'it must

be tiring having all those babies.' And I can tell she's getting really upset now. I walk over to her with Chip and give her a one-armed hug.

'No, she wasn't even the puppies' mother. It was just any old dog,' says Marcus. Mum's face breaks.

'Marcus, stop it now, you are spoiling everything. Chip is a beautiful little puppy and this is meant to be the happiest day of my life,' I say.

'Delilah, don't you see?' Marcus pleads with me. 'Chip don't know what a washing machine is, and he don't know what a TV is, and he don't know what anything is, because he is not a dog from a family home.'

Mum goes to twiddle with her bracelet but of course her wrist is bare so she starts wringing her hands instead.

The cold doubt rises and rises, exploding out of my mouth.

'GET OUT, MARCUS! How can you spoil this day? My first ever day with my new puppy.'

'I've got paperwork,' says Mum, marching over to the drawer in the sideboard, whisking out a folder and waving it in the air. 'George was a very nice man, how could you say such things?'

'It's not even his real name,' says Marcus.

Chip is trembling. 'Marcus, just go. You are scaring my puppy.'

'He didn't even ask your mum about her home, they didn't even check if Chip was going to a loving family, they just wanted her money. You *know* that's not right.'

'You're just jealous you haven't got a dog of your own. At this moment I hate you, Marcus Sparrow.'

'But Delilah—'

'HOME NOW, I WANT WORDS WITH YOU,' says Nana. 'I've never been so ashamed. I can only apologise, Florence and Delilah. I can promise you, Marcus has not been brought up to break into peoples' houses.'

As they leave, I take Chip into my bedroom and lie on my bed. He lets out a tiny whimper. He is very still.

16

Marcus

I sit in my thinking place in the garden as the evening starts to darken, Nana's telling-off still scorching my ears.

Delilah hates me and everything is rubbish.

I text her.

Friends?

I wait and wait, but there is no reply.

Pleeeeease?

A wet nose pushes through the hole in the fence.

'Moon Dog,' I breathe.

I put out my hand and Moon Dog rests his chin on it. We sit there for ages, dog and boy, boy and dog – except there is a horrible great fence between us. As it grows darker, there is still no sign of the men, and even with Nana's threats still ringing in my ears, I can't help myself – I climb over, praying that Nana Sparrow does not see me.

Moon Dog wags his tail as he stands really close to me, pressing his body into my legs as I stroke his soft black coat.

There is still no sign of life from the house. I find a stick for Moon Dog and throw it to play fetch. But he does not know what to do. I don't think the men play with him, so I run and get the stick myself and Moon Dog bounds after me. I don't like the taste of wood in my mouth, so we play chase instead and roll on the ground together, me and Moon Dog, Moon Dog and me. I pretend I am at a dog show, and run round the outside of the grass as if it's a show ring, and Moon Dog is the champion. Yaaaaay! The crowd cheers as we do our lap of honour. It is now really dark.

'MARCUS, GET IN HERE,' a voice bellows through the dark.

It's Nana Sparrow, calling me in to bed. I

pray that she doesn't come into our garden and see that I'm not there, but does her usual thing of just shouting from the kitchen without even bothering to open the door. It's all that shouting at her market stall – that's given her good practice. *Spuds, two bags for the price of one. And apples, come get your apples and pears*. Nana Sparrow is the best shouter in London.

My quilt is still in Moon Dog's shelter, so I make him comfortable.

'Good night, Moon Dog.' I put my arms around this giant of all dogs, and hug him. He licks my cheek.

'MAAAAARCUS, BED TIME.'

I run for the fence and scramble over, and zoom in through the back door.

Nana is watching TV; she doesn't even look up. She's still vexed with me.

I check my phone. Still no reply from Delilah.

I trudge with sad, heavy steps upstairs to bed.

It's the middle of the night. My phone bleeps.

> **Chip sick please come**

I was sleeping, but Delilah's text means I'm now wide awake. My blood is pounding.

I leap out of bed and go to knock on Nana's door.

'Nana, Nana, wake up.'

Nana Sparrow opens the door in her nightdress. She does not look happy. 'What's all this racket?'

'It's Delilah. Her puppy's sick.' I show her my phone.

Nana sighs. 'I'll get dressed, we'd best get round there.'

I pause outside Dad's room. I want to wake him. I want him to tell me what to do. I want him to be a dad. I lift up my hand to knock, but let it flop back by my side. What's the point? He'll be useless. Nothing will get him out of bed. Nothing.

I text Delilah.

> **Coming with Nana**

Ten minutes later, we are driving through the night.

'Nana,' I say, 'what if . . .'

'Marcus, you are going to have to be very strong for your friend; she has been through so much.'

When we get to the fourth floor of the Beckham Estate, Delilah's front door is propped open.

'Hello,' calls Nana.

'Come through,' answers Florence from inside the flat.

A foul smell hits my nostrils as I walk through the door. It's like blood mixed with metal.

Chip is lying on a blanket, with Delilah curled up next to him.

I can see his belly is really bloated. The little puppy has been sick, and messed himself and I can see that there is some blood in the poo.

Florence has rubber gloves on and is cleaning up.

Delilah looks up at me, such desperate fright in her eyes.

'Marcus, I don't know what to do. Tell me what to do.'

'Matt the Vet should be here soon,' Florence tells us. 'He is doing an emergency night call. He was very kind and said under the circumstances . . .'

Fear grips my belly; this does not look good.

'Delilah,' says Nana, 'keep talking to Chip.'

'Yes,' I say, 'he knows you love him. Keep talking, so he can hear your voice.'

'Chip,' says Delilah, 'you listen to me, little boy, you get better now, because we are going to have so much fun on our walks, you, me and Marcus. And we'll teach you our song.' And she starts singing 'Lead Walking'.

And I join in because Delilah is sobbing.

'Hello, it's Matt, can I come in?' a voice calls out.

'Please, come on through,' calls Florence.

Matt walks into the front room, takes one look at the scene and swoops down on his knees next to Delilah and Chip.

Delilah has gone oh-so still, her eyes on Chip, and a blanket of silence has come down on the room.

Matt takes a stethoscope out of his bag, and listens to Chip's chest, whilst leaning over him. I think he is listening for breathing. He straightens up and taps the corner of the puppy's eye, but Chip does not blink. He stares into space.

Matt shakes his head.

'I am afraid his little heart has stopped. Your Chip has slipped away. He was a very sick little dog but he is not suffering now. He is at peace.'

'No! Please, Chip, wake up, wake up, little one.'

'Delilah,' whispers Florence, pulling her daughter close. 'Darling, he's gone.'

'Noooooooo, noooooo,' howls Delilah. She shakes herself free and runs into her bedroom.

'Delilah,' calls Florence.

I follow her and watch as she ducks into her tepee book-den.

I am gritting my teeth so hard, because I can't cry in front of Delilah. I must hold it together for her, but my heart feels like it's ripped in two.

Nana Sparrow takes me by the arm and leads me back to the front room. 'Let Delilah have a private moment.'

'I am certain it's parvo, from the smell,' says Matt. 'I need to take Chip with me, to do some tests.'

Florence has sunk down on the sofa, wringing her hands.

'Where did you get Chip from?' asks Matt.

And I tell the vet about Nose Ring and Leopard Tattoo, of all I saw and heard when I hid in the chest, and how Chip and his brothers and sisters behaved nothing like Smee, Peter Pan, Wendy, Tinker Bell and Tiger Lily. I tell him about the phones with different names, numbers and dog breeds, of the strange room with the different wallpapers, and I tell them of the dog with no name, who I named Moon Dog under the silvery moon.

'Illegal puppy sellers,' he says. 'These people are unscrupulous. To them, a puppy is not a living thing with feelings, but just a means of making money. Mrs Jones, I need to do a post-mortem on Chip, to prove it's parvovirus, so that it can be used as evidence against these men. I do need to take him.'

'Yes, right,' says Florence, looking completely broken. 'I should have done more research. I should have asked questions. I can't believe I was stupid enough to be taken in.'

Matt puts his hand on Florence's arm. 'These people are evil and they play on people's emotions. They need stopping,' he says.

'Let me get Delilah,' Nana Sparrow says. 'She needs to come and say goodbye to Chip properly. It's important.'

In her room, Delilah is still howling in her book den.

I have to find a way to reach her in her sadness.

'Please, darling, come out,' says Florence. 'You need to say goodbye to Chip.'

'No,' says Delilah. 'I can't.'

'Come on,' says Nana. 'Be a brave girl.'

'No,' Delilah is shouting now. 'No, no, no. This can't be happening . . . First Dad, then my dog. I can't let Chip go too. I need him.'

A tear trickles down Florence's cheek. 'Oh, my little girl,' she whispers.

192

'Delilah.' I lie on my belly in front of the closed flap entrance to the tepee. 'Listen to me. They are two separate things, and two such hard things to deal with, I can see that, but please do not lump them into one big thing, because that's too heavy for anyone to carry. I know your dad is watching over you. At this moment, saying goodbye to Chip is what you need to do. Please come out.'

'Give me eleven reasons why,' she sobs.

I take a deep breath.

'One: you can't stay in your book den for ever.'

'I can,' she says, 'just watch me.'

'Two . . .' I look around the room, and see the little dog bed in the corner. 'I think Chip should be laid to rest in his sky-blue dog bed. It will be like he's floating on a cloud. It will be a lovely place of rest for him.'

Florence runs out of the room and comes back carrying a shirt. She shoves it in my hand and whispers, 'This was her dad's.'

'Three: your mum's just given me one of your dad's shirts, and we can line the dog bed with it, and then Chip will know your dad's scent, and they will find each other in heaven and both watch over you.'

'Four: in his short, short life, Chip has touched me and my nana and your mum, and we would all like the chance to say goodbye to him. But we can't do that without you. Please, Delilah.'

'Yes, I would very much like to say goodbye to the little fellow,' says Nana Sparrow, 'but with you by my side, Delilah.'

'Five: Matt needs to examine Chip to see what happened to him, and you need to say goodbye so he can do this.'

'Six: Matt needs to do this because these men and their lies need to be stopped.'

'Seven: by helping Matt, you will help other sick puppies, and Chip's short life will mean something.'

'Eight: it will be a step towards gathering evidence to stop these men.'

'Nine: you can be the one to help stop other kids from going through this heartbreak.'

'Ten: your dad would be so proud of you.'

'Eleven . . .' I take a deep breath. 'Delilah, you are brave and tremendous.'

The blanket of silence comes down again as we all watch and wait.

The flap of the tepee twitches.

Delilah's tiny hand pokes out and grabs the tepee flap and, pushing it to one side, out she crawls, cradling her red beanie hat and a blue rabbit toy.

I give Delilah a hug and hold her hand, leading her back to the front room to have her last moment with Chip.

Delilah puts little Chip inside her red beanie hat.

'To keep him warm,' she says, and Matt helps her lay him in the sky-blue dog bed, and she ruffles her dad's shirt round him.

'I want him to have blue rabbit, that my Dad bought me to cuddle,' says Delilah, and she puts the cuddly toy next to the little puppy, and we all say goodbye to Chip.

17

Marcus

It's four o'clock in the morning.

I can still hear Delilah crying in her bedroom, like her heart is broken, and will never ever mend.

My legs feel as heavy as elephants, and no words come. What is there left to say? It feels like everything is happening a long way away.

Florence is rummaging in a drawer.

'Ah, here it is.' She walks over to Matt with documents in her hand. 'This is the paperwork that came with Chip.'

'Thank you,' says Matt. 'I'll look over it, but I very much doubt these documents are worth the paper they're written on.'

'I was well and truly taken in,' says Florence,

shaking her head.

'As, sadly, are many thousands of people,' says Matt. He pauses before saying, 'I know that this is the last thing on your mind, but the parvovirus will have contaminated this flat so you need to clean it as soon as possible. Unfortunately, bleach isn't enough to kill this deadly virus, so I'll send over a special cleaning solution to use. In the meantime, you are going to have to get rid of the clothes you are wearing, and any soft furnishings the puppy has come in contact with – so, carpet, cushions, bedding. All of that, I'm afraid.'

Florence sinks down on to the sofa, looking shocked.

Matt pats her arm. 'I'll check up on both of you tomorrow, if that's OK? I can go through it all again then. Go get some rest.'

We go down in the lift, our sad party of three: Nana Sparrow, Matt and me. Matt has his veterinary bag slung over his shoulder, and he is holding the sky-blue dog bed, with little Chip, who is no longer suffering, lying in peace.

197

'I need to take Chip back to my surgery now, but would you mind if I came round to yours afterwards, Mrs Sparrow? I would like to take a look at Moon Dog if he's there, from over your back garden fence.'

'Of course,' says Nana Sparrow. 'I'll make us all a spot of breakfast.'

'You can use my crates to climb over,' I say.

'No, I don't have authority to go into next door's garden, but it would help to see the set-up. We need as much evidence as we can gather on these men and their shady operation.'

We nod our goodbyes and Nana marches over to our van. I trudge on my elephant legs behind her.

Nana turns and looks back at me.

'Marcus, I don't have the words to say how proud I am of you tonight. Now come on, slow-coach.'

Oh my goodness! If I had any energy I would run and hug Nana, but instead I just give her a tired almost-grin.

As we drive towards Mabel Street, the wind

blows through the open window and starts to wake up my senses.

Nana parks the van. The FOR SALE sign is firmly stuck in the ground outside the house next door.

We need to wash and get rid of these clothes we've worn, like Matt said. We cannot risk spreading parvovirus.

Half an hour later, in fresh tracksuit bottoms and T-shirt, I rush to answer the door to Matt.

'Look,' I say, pointing to the FOR SALE sign. 'They keep moving the sign all the time and one of the men works in Grayson & Stoat estate agents.'

'You're a smart boy, Marcus,' he says. 'You'd make an excellent detective.'

Even though I'm sad, I feel this mad grin on my face that Matt, who is an actual vet, thinks I'm smart.

Nana goes straight to work in the kitchen. As I lead Matt out through the back door, I tell him about Moon Dog and how clever he is, but when we look over the fence, Moon Dog has gone.

The garden is empty apart from my quilt, lying there with muddy paw prints all over it. The house is deserted, with staring windows.

'Moon Dog comes and he goes,' I say. 'Mostly I see him by moonlight. I felt a callous on his elbow, I think from sleeping on hard ground in the shelter. I've given him my quilt off my bed, though don't tell Nana Sparrow, please.'

Matt laughs and puts his finger to his lips. 'Promise I won't,' he says.

'Oh dear,' says Matt, looking up at next door's house. 'They are clever, these con men, breeding puppies for man's greedy profit, with no thought for the dogs' welfare.'

We go into the kitchen, and there is a big pile of bacon sandwiches in the middle of the table. Matt tucks in. At least bacon sandwiches are normal food, and he's not having to put up with Nana's mad cooking.

Even though I am starving, I can hardly swallow, as all I can think about is where my Moon Dog is and when I will see him again.

Over the weekend, I text Delilah.

How r u you doing?

No reply.

Do u want 2 talk?

No reply

Would u like me 2 come round?

But she still doesn't reply.

I race to school on Monday and wait by the school gate for her.

Luckily for me, as Sol, Nico and Baz swagger into school, Mr Lawson is waiting for them. Something to do with graffiti in the boys' toilets. It says *BEWARE OF THE GOST CHILDRIN*. Word has it he knew it was them because of the spelling, but I'm not really interested to be honest.

'Soon, Big M, soon,' whispers Nico, as the head marches him past me. But I just ignore him. I haven't got even a tiny bit of space left in my brain to worry about the Cinder Street Boyz when my friend is so sad.

I give up waiting for Delilah, but as I walk past the library I see her in there, in deep conversation with Miss Raquel. She must have got to school really, really early. I don't want to interrupt their private talk and realise I'm going to be late for my lesson, so I rush off down the corridor. It's boring geography, followed by boring history. Everything is just boring without Delilah by my side.

By lunchtime I have had enough.

I see Delilah, still in the library, with Wilbur.

'Delilah!' I barge in. 'Please don't cut me out. Talk to me. Come lead walking with me.'

Delilah looks crushed.

'Lead walking? How can you be so insensitive? How . . . ?'

'No!' I say, realising what she's thinking. 'Delilah . . . I didn't mean . . . We can do a walk, in memory of Chip. We . . . we could scatter flowers on the heath, to say goodbye.'

Wilbur stands on his hind legs and nudges Delilah with his nose.

'See, Wilbur knows you are sad, and he thinks you should go.'

Slowly, slowly a shadow of a smile appears

on Delilah's face. 'OK then, this evening. I will meet you at Rose Manor Hall at seven.'

'I will bring the flowers. Chip was your dog,' I say, 'and he knew it, he died knowing he was loved.'

I hold my hand out, and she presses her tiny hand against my palm.

'See you later,' I say.

18

Marcus

I rush home after school and change into my best black trousers and white shirt that I wore to Mum's cousin's wedding. I also put on my black bow-tie, as a finishing touch. I want to look respectful for Chip's memory walk.

I empty my jar of 1ps and 2ps, and go to the flower stall next to Nana Sparrow's stall. Nana is haggling over a bunch of carrots.

There seem to be a lot of carrots on the stall. Oh, no! Carrot pancakes were an all-time low, but I like carrot cake.

I know that Delilah loves the colours sky-blue and red, so I choose red poppies and bluebells.

'Who are those for?' Nana shouts over.

'I am taking Delilah on a memory walk for

Chip,' I shout back.

'Oh, that's kind, Marcus. Here you go.' And she gives me ten pounds from the money bag she wears on a belt around her waist.

I make my way to the heath, carrying the massive bunch of flowers. It's a lovely evening, still and warm.

I am ten minutes early when I reach the top of the hill. I sit on a low, old brick wall that once must have been part of the entrance hall to Rose Manor Hall, to wait for Delilah.

Moon Dog thoughts flood my brain. Where is he when he's not next door? Supposing he's cold at night? Supposing he's not got enough to eat? Supposing he's really missing me, supposing—

'Got you!' Sol, Nico and Baz surround me.

'Ah! Got all dressed up for your initiation into the Cinder Street Boyz, have you?' says Sol, and they start to laugh.

'No,' I say.

'Who are those flowers for? Your little girlfriend?' says Baz, making to grab them.

'No, please.' I hold them out of reach. Which

is easy to do as I am so much taller than Baz.

'Saw your granny today, selling her skanky fruit and veg,' says Nico.

My anger match strikes. 'Don't talk that way about my nana.'

'Yeah,' says Baz, 'and Mummy ran away, didn't she? Didn't want you no more.'

My belly fills with fire.

'And your dad,' says Sol. 'What a joke he is! What a mess. What an embarrassment.'

I explode.

'Don't you—'

'Yeah, Big M,' they all start shouting.

'Yeah, you are well and truly goaded. We need your anger, Big M,' shouts Sol.

'We've told you what your initiation is. Kick that high wall down, like what we said. If you do, you're one of us,' says Nico, and I drop the flowers, and start to kick.

'Go on! Harder!' shouts Baz, and I do, I kick harder. I can't take it no more. I feel like my brain is going to explode.

The Cinder Steet Boyz are hollering and

whooping me on.

'Yeah, Big M. Go on, BIG M.'

Kick, kick, kick and the wall starts to crumble.

'Yeah!' I shout and look up.

Delilah is standing there, staring at me in horror. And I think what this must look like to her.

'How could you do this? It's Chip's memory day. You lied. Liar, Liar. Liar. You said these boys weren't your friends. How can you destroy our wondrous place? I trusted you, Marcus.'

'No, Delilah, please.' And I scrabble on the floor for the flowers. 'Look, I bought these for Chip.'

'I thought you were my friend,' shouts Delilah, 'but you're nothing but a thug. I hate you.' And she runs off.

'Delilah,' I call after her, but she has gone.

And I feel so empty.

The sound of splintering wood and stones smashing through brick bounces around me, as Baz, Sol and Nico smash up the ruins of Rose Manor Hall.

Through clouds of dust, I see two men running towards us.

As they get closer, I realise it's Leopard Tattoo and Nose Ring.

'Oy! Nico,' shouts Leopard Tattoo. 'I paid you to keep kids away from here. You wait till I get hold of you.'

'Run,' yells Nico.

I follow Baz, Sol and Nico down the hill. I stumble forward over a boulder, falling flat on my face. As I look up, I see the Cinder Street Boyz are now far ahead, abandoning me in their desperation to get away. And as they disappear into the distance, so too does my fear of them. I will never do what they tell me ever again. They are gone from my life.

I roll behind a bush, holding my breath, but the men haven't seen me. They run past, after the gang.

Peeping between the twigs and leaves, I see the clump of faraway trees the Cinder Street Boyz vanished into, and the two men giving up and walking, puffing and panting, back up the hill towards me.

As they get nearer, I hear them talking.

'I gave Nico cash to spread the story of the ghost children, to keep people away from here. I am going to kill him,' says Leopard Tattoo.

'Yeah, we can't have anyone near here, too risky,' says Nose Ring.

Why would he want Nico to spread the story of the ghost children? This doesn't make sense, but those thoughts are quickly squashed in my mind by my Moon Dog worries. I have to find out what they have done with him.

I wait and watch till the men have gone past me, then I follow them back up the hill, ducking and diving behind trees, so as not to be seen. Maybe they will lead me to Moon Dog.

Leopard Tattoo kicks away some gravel and reaches down and pulls up a metal manhole cover, and I watch as both men disappear down through the hole in the ground.

My big feet are itching to follow them, but suppose the men catch me and trap me underground? So I watch and wait, and wait, and wait for what seems like for ever, feeling cut-up to my very core that Delilah thinks I am a liar and a thug.

The night starts to fall, and birds call into the dusk. I shiver as a breeze swirls round me. I wish I'd worn my jacket. Then just as I think I will be hiding behind the bush for ever, first one man, then the other, appears out of the hole in the ground. Leopard Tattoo replaces the manhole cover, and kicks gravel and earth back over it. They both disappear into the night.

I run to the spot and, kneeling down, I scrabble in the earth until my hand clasps the handle of the manhole cover. Pulling it up with all my strength, I drop it to one side. I pull my mobile out of my pocket and, turning the torch on, shine it down the hole, on to a rusty metal ladder that disappears into darkness.

I put my phone between my teeth and start to climb down, down, down into the deep hole.

19

Marcus

The cold, rusty metal digs into my hands as I make my way slowly, one foot at a time, down the long, long ladder. I just have to hope there's no one else down here, now that the two men have gone, 'cause even though I am trying my best to be careful, my big feet make such a clanging noise as I climb down.

Over the clang, clang, clang of my feet, I can hear a faint whimpering. Supposing it's the ghost children? And then I remember that was just a story to keep kids away from here. My fear is playing tricks on me.

'Get a grip, Marcus,' I mutter to myself – which is hard, let me tell you, as I am biting my phone between my teeth – and my mumbled voice sounds so strange, it makes me jump. I can also hear what sounds like an echoing of dogs barking, but a long way away.

At last, I reach the bottom of the ladder. Grabbing my phone from my mouth, I shine the light down the dark, narrow tunnel in front of me, and start feeling my way along the rough rock walls. On top of the smell of the cold damp air is a foul odour that's getting stronger, and makes my nostrils flare. The barking gets louder and louder. Surely there can't be dogs down here in this terrible place? Reaching an old wooden door with metal studs as large as saucers, I stretch up to a massive bolt, draw it back and enter.

A wall of noise hits me, and as I shine the light from my phone round this underground cellar, I see puppies. Puppies everywhere, in cages! It's not ghost children whimpering, it's dogs! Dachshunds, Jack Russells, poodles, shih tzu, cockapoos, Jugs, pugs, chihuahuas, French bulldogs, Cavaliers. All in cages that are piled high on top of each other.

The puppies are so young, some of them just squeak and whimper, or stand stock still, silently staring with wild, terrified eyes, or peeping at me through filthy straw. Some cages just have sawdust, and none has proper bedding and it's so cold and dark down here.

'It's all right, little ones,' I say. 'I am Marcus, please don't be frightened, I won't hurt you.'

As I walk through the huge cellar I realise the dogs in the cages are gradually getting older until I am swallowed into a wall of barking. Snarling dogs, howling dogs, yapping dogs. Dogs walking backwards and forwards, backwards and forwards, dogs cowering in corners. Dogs weaving and spinning round and round, trapped in the four walls of their metal cages.

The smell of wee makes my eyes water and my throat itch, but the smell of dog poo is even worse and makes me gag. Every so often, I am hit with the stench of blood and metal, like I smelt at Delilah's. Parvo!

This is like a nightmare version of *101*

Dalmatians, only it's not cute cartoon dogs, it's living, breathing puppies. This must be a real-life puppy farm; I've seen terrible places like this on the news. I remember Matt's words, *Breeding puppies for man's greedy profit, with no thought for the dogs' welfare.*

I come to another closed door. I try to open it, but it's wedged shut. Putting all my weight against it, I manage to shove it open a little way, and squeeze through, thankful to be putting my strength to something useful rather than smashing things up. The room has lots of wooden boxes. Red heat lamps glow in the dark, fixed to the top of the boxes.

My phone is down to two bars, and I don't want the battery to run out, so I turn it off and put it back in my pocket. I lean over one of the boxes. The terrified eyes of a Cavalier King Charles spaniel stares up at me in the red light. She is surrounded by five tiny pups. Her black-and-tan coat is matted and dirty. There are no blankets, just a cold stone floor.

'Hello, girl.'

She's shaking. My heart tears into bits.

'Please don't be frightened,' I say, 'I won't hurt you. I am your friend Marcus.'

But she doesn't know what kind words are. She doesn't know what love is, and shakes harder.

In each of the boxes, there's a different breed of mother dog – a bulldog, a beagle, a cockapoo, and so on. Some with pups, some with swollen bellies, waiting to give birth in this hell.

So it looks like some of the puppies are born here, and some smuggled in from outside. This is a huge criminal operation.

Poor little Chip didn't stand a chance.

I back away into the centre of the room in horror.

'I will find a way to get you all out of here, as sure as my name is Marcus Sparrow,' I shout, over the barking.

'Oh, will you now?'

I spin round. It's Leopard Tattoo.

'Well, we'll see about that.' And he grabs my arms with brute force, and pins them behind me. I struggle as he drags me backwards and pushes me through a door at the back of the room.

'Please don't leave me in here,' I plead as he slams the door. I hear the key turning in the lock.

Then the sound of laughter and echoing footsteps as he walks away, through the barking dogs.

'Come back,' I call, 'don't leave me here.'

My legs feel all shaky. I flop on to the floor, pulling my knees close to me and start to rock to try to keep the cold out.

Something furry nudges into me. A nose pushes into my hand and a string of warm slobber hits me in the face. It's Moon Dog! My Moon Dog. As I fling my arms round him, burying my face into his beautiful black fur, braveness pours into me. Now I am not alone; my Moon Dog is by my side. I have to find a way to get us out of here. I just have to.

20

Marcus

I feel for my phone in my pocket and switch it on.

Moon Dog sniffs it. His coat feels damp.

'Moon Dog,' I say. 'I'm going to try and text Delilah. Do you think she'll forgive me?'

He licks my cheek.

But I have no signal!

I shake my phone. Still nothing. I switch it off and shove it back in my pocket. I could do with the phone torch, but I can't risk the battery running out. I scramble up, and walk slowly, step by step, around the dark room. Moon Dog stays next to me, pressing into my legs. I put my hand on his head. The sound of all those dogs, barking, barking, barking, clangs in my brain. The smell sickens my belly. The cold makes my bones shrink.

I stumble over something and fall forwards, putting my hands out to save myself. One hand hits the stone-cold floor, the other, wood. Moon Dog whimpers and starts licking me everywhere, his slobber dripping on to my face.

'I'm OK, boy,' I say. 'I'm not hurt.'

Moon Dog nudges me with his nose, and I haul myself up. I feel in the dark to see what I fell over. It's a broken chair, fallen on its side. I walk with Moon Dog towards the back of the room. Step by step, reaching the right-hand corner. I feel for my phone in my pocket and switch it on. I've got one bar of signal. I look up, and there's a tiny sliver of light coming through a crack in the ceiling. I text,

Delilah please help me

I press send. I decide it's best to send lots of short messages, in case the signal goes again, and there's more chance of at least one of them getting through.

I wait and wait. No reply.

Delilah am stuck in cellar of Rose Manor Hall

Still nothing.

Then my phone bleeps.

Marcus get lost. Stop messing with my head

I reply,

**I'm not messing, am with M Dog
HELP**

I press send.

Phone bleeps.

**I mean it Marcus, GO AWAY
I thought u were my friend
U R not
U r nothing 2 me**

I swallow and swallow. I mustn't cry. Moon Dog licks my cheek.

I remember the day that Delilah came into my life. That first day, when I put my big foot out, so that she could climb on to the high stool in art class.

Then I think of the words she said to me that day, and start texting,

**U OWE ME
I AM NOT MESSING
I AM UNDERGROUND WITH
M DOG & 100 PUPPIES**

WE NEED U 2 RESCUE US
DO IT 4 CHIP

I spend the next two hours cuddled up to Moon Dog for warmth, turning my phone on and off to check for messages. But still nothing, nothing, nothing from Delilah.

In the cold and the dark, I begin to think about my mum and about how she has no idea that her only son, Marcus Sparrow, is being held captive. Maybe if she knew, she would come and get me. But then I realise that she doesn't care where I am or what I'm doing. She made that clear when she left. Then my thoughts flip to Dad lying in bed. What use is he?

My anger match strikes, filling me with fire, but it also burns brightly with anger for all those dogs out there, barking in the dark in this underground hell, and I am filled with rage for this beautiful Newfoundland dog, who is owned by those men. A dog with no name, except to me.

'Moon Dog, Moon Dog, Moon Dog,' I whisper the name I have given him into his ear again and again. As I do, I start to breathe out anger and breathe in love.

I breathe out my mum, who has chosen not to be in my life, and I breathe in Nana Sparrow, who cares for me, day in and day out. My nana will be worried sick. I breathe in my dad, who loves me, I am sure, even though he spends his life in the bed with a leg made of books.

If I ever get out of here, maybe one day when I am older, I can go and find Mum and introduce myself, but it's getting home to my nana and my dad, who love and care for me now, that matters.

'HELP! LET ME OUT,' I shout over the barking dogs.

But there is no one there to hear me. I am so hungry I would even gobble up one of Nana's cauliflower fritters.

My thoughts tick over in the dark. Leopard Tattoo works at Grayson & Stoat, so he knew that Mr Anderson's empty house was the perfect place to dress up as a family home and sell puppies from, what with Mr Anderson being in Hong Kong, and too far away to check up on his old house. And, well, it's obvious that Leopard Tattoo made sure that the house wasn't sold. Their finishing touch was paying Nico to keep the myth of the ghost children alive, to keep people away from Rose Manor Hall so that they didn't hear the puppies' cries. A genius criminal plan!

My phone bleeps.

On my way
Where are u?

'She's coming, Moon Dog. Delilah's coming!'
I text,

Come 2 Rose Manor Hall

Near where your flowers r on ground
U will see climbing rose & honeysuckle

There is manhole cover underneath gravel
Go down ladder

Me & M Dog in cellar at end

Then I cuddle up to my Moon Dog to wait.

21

Delilah

As I march over the heath, I am still fuming at Marcus. But I owe him, and I always, always pay my debts, so I snuck out of the flat while Mum was sound asleep. Can he really be stuck under the ground, with a hundred puppies and Moon Dog? That don't make sense to me.

My steps are heavy with sadness walking on the heath, knowing that I will never walk with Chip by my side. The night-time trees look like they are stretching out twig fingers to snatch me up. If you ask me, it's properly spooky on the heath at two in the morning.

By the light of my phone torch, I stomp up the hill towards the dark skeleton of Rose Manor Hall, quick as quick, one-two, one-two, to keep warm. I hear the faintest of whimpering on the breeze. Ghost children! But if what Marcus says is true, then it's not ghost children at all, but puppies. My foot slips. I shine the light down, and see the red petals, mashed into the grass, marking the spot where Marcus ripped my heart into bits.

'Don't think about that now, Delilah,' I say, into the cold night air.

I hear the sound of an engine getting closer. I turn round to see a van bumping over the grass. No headlights – so they don't want to be seen. I duck behind a bush and watch. To be honest, I am glad to stop for a moment; a cloak of tiredness wraps itself around me.

The van drives past and stops right in front of my hiding place. The back of the van is only a giant's arm-stretch in front of the very bush I am crouching behind. In fact, I bet Marcus would be able to reach out and touch it. Thinking of Marcus hurts too much. I swallow.

I hold my breath as I peep through the twigs. The burly driver opens the van door and leaps on to the grass and waits, as two men come towards him in the dark. The smallest one switches on a torch. I slam my hand over my mouth, stopping my gasp. It's Nose Ring and Leopard Tattoo, the hateful men that Mum bought Chip from.

They move round to the back of the van and open the doors. An owl hoots, and I shudder as something scurries over my foot. The burly driver moves a wall of boxes that are hiding a stack of cages. He reaches in and brings one out, and I shove my whole fist in my mouth, to stop myself crying out. It's full of tiny puppies. Cage upon cage of frightened puppies, just like Marcus said, and by the look of them, too young to be away from their mothers. Poor little things! How long have they been crammed together in the back of the van like that – frightened, with no idea of where they are going, breathing in all the fumes and the dust and nowhere to have a wee except in the cage, all over each other. This is so cruel! My heart breaks at the thought of Chip making such a frightening journey.

Nose-Ring Man pulls a wad of notes out of his pocket.

'It's all there,' he says, handing it to the van driver, who grabs it and shoves the money inside his jacket.

I watch as they walk by torchlight to the space that Marcus described in his text, between the climbing rose and the honeysuckle.

Leopard-Tattoo Man kicks some gravel aside, and reaches down and pulls up an iron manhole cover. The three men start carrying the cages out of the van, and disappear down into the ground. Cage upon cage. My legs feel as if they will seize up, and I will be stuck in a crouching position for the rest of my life. I rock backwards on to my bottom, the night dew seeping through my jeans to my knickers. Yuck!

I hug my knees to my chest and watch and wait and wait and wait, gathering my energy again for what lies ahead. After what seems like for ever, the van is empty. The three men go round to the other side of the van, and start talking.

'What are you going to do with the boy?' I hear a gruff voice say. 'He can't stay there – the police will be looking for him.'

'We need to shut him up,' says another voice.

I shiver. Marcus is in danger. I need to act NOW.

I sprint across the grass, past the other side of the van so I'm not seen, to the hole in the ground. I find the top rung of the ladder with my foot, and start to climb down, down, down.

I hear a clang above me. One of the men is climbing down the ladder too!

I speed up, left-right, left-right and nearly miss my footing. Grabbing the ladder with all my strength, my heart hammering, I continue down, and at last I reach the ground. I switch my phone torch on and run down the tunnel that stretches out ahead of me. I hear the clanging of the man from above, still climbing down the ladder, getting closer. There is an open wooden door, and I run through it, towards the barking, so loud I feel it will shatter my bones. And the smell, oh, the smell! My eyes sting, my throat itches and burns from the smell of wee and poo and then I retch as I smell that same smell from when my little Chip . . . I have to pause for a moment as I think of my poor, poor little boy.

In the dark, lots and lots of eyes are staring at me. Cage upon cage of scared puppies. The footsteps are getting nearer. The only place to hide is in with the puppies.

I undo the front of the end cage, turn my phone

torch off, and crawl into the cage with a litter of cockapoos, curling up in a ball at the back, praying that the man doesn't see me. I feel the little pups sniffling at me. A beam of light and Leopard-Tattoo Man walks past carrying a lamp. He hasn't seen me. I breathe.

'It's OK, little ones,' I whisper into the dark, but they cower, frightened at my words.

Marcus's text said he was imprisoned in a cellar at the end.

Leopard Tattoo squeezes through a gap in a wedged-open door ahead. Maybe he will lead me to Marcus. I clamber out of the cage and run and peep round the gap. I see lots of wooden boxes, red lamps above them glowing in the dark, and I see the man unlock a door at the end and drag it open.

I get a brief glimpse of Marcus, huddled in the dark, with Moon Dog next to him, before the door slams shut. I thank all the stars in the sky that at least now I know where they are trapped. But I am their only hope of escape, and that is a very scary thought.

I dash into the room and duck behind the nearest box.

I hear the man shout over the barking, 'Here, eat this.'

'LET ME OUT.'

It's Marcus shouting and sounding oh-so frightened!

'THE POLICE WILL BE LOOKING FOR ME.'

I hear a low rumbling growl. It must be Moon Dog.

'YOU ARE NOT GOING ANYWHERE,' shouts the man. 'SHUT UP, DOG.'

Leopard Tattoo opens the door again, leaving Marcus and Moon Dog in their prison. I sink back into the dark, damp corner, behind the box, as he marches back past me, squeezes through the gap in the door and is gone.

As soon as the coast is clear, I pull myself up and lock eyes with a shih tzu sitting under a red heat lamp. Her haunted stare glares up at me from a filthy, tangled, matted coat of fur. Her huge belly full of puppies. I have to find a way to help these dogs. Each and every one of them.

'Don't be frightened, little one,' I whisper. 'We will find a way to get you out of here.'

I run past all the breeding boxes to the locked door at the end of the room. 'Marcus,' I hiss. 'It's me.'

'Delilah! I knew you would come! Please get me out of here.'

I switch my phone torch on, and shine it up the wall. There is actually a gap between the top of the door and the wall, and there are these studs sticking out of the wood. I reckon my feet are small enough to use them as a ladder.

'Marcus, I'm going to try and climb the door and squeeze through that gap at the top.'

'Be careful, Delilah,' Marcus calls out.

I put my foot on the first stud. It comes away from the door in a cloud of rust. I start again, bending my knee to my chest, so my foot is high enough to reach the stud above. It holds. I reach up and, clasping the stud above that one, I haul myself up, bit by bit, one foot, then the other, until I reach the top. I push my head and shoulders through the gap.

Marcus and Moon Dog are staring up at me in the dim light of the lamp.

'Don't just stand there,' I hiss.

Marcus runs to the door, and reaches up, up, up

and I wriggle further through, and reach down, down, down till our fingertips touch.

'Don't move,' says Marcus, and runs to a broken-looking chair, lying on its side. He drags it over to the door and steps on it, and grabs my wrists. I wriggle further through the gap.

I am upside down now, face against the door.

I feel arms round my waist, and hear the sound of the splintering chair, as Marcus swings me down and round, and we land in a heap on the floor. Moon Dog licks my face.

Marcus jumps to his feet and pulls me up into a hug, but I push him away.

'I've not forgiven you, Marcus Sparrow.'

'Delilah, I'm so sorry. I lied to you, those boys have been plaguing me ever since I've known you, and tonight they pushed all my buttons, and I got caught in a situation.'

I give him my best poison-eye arrows.

'You can't hate me as much as I hate myself, because I would never disrespect you or Chip's memory. You are my only friend. I would do anything for you, Delilah.'

I feel my heart ice melt, just a trickle.

'No time for soppy stuff,' I say, 'we've got to get out of here.'

'How?' asks Marcus.

'Well, there's got to be another way out of this room,' I say.

'How do you know?'

'Duh,' I say, 'because Moon Dog didn't climb down the ladder, did he? What, you think one of those men gave him a piggyback down?'

'Oh, yeah.' He shrugs his shoulders, and scuffs his foot on the floor, then looks up and grins, and I try my best to stop my grin back at him, but it escapes and I feel my lips twitch.

'We've gotta find the other entrance,' I say.

'You know what?' says Marcus. 'Nana Sparrow told me Rose Manor Hall is so old that it was even standing in the times of Guy Fawkes and that legend goes that he planned to watch Parliament burn from the top of the hill. I bet you anything there's a secret passage in this house so that Guy Fawkes and his men could escape from the soldiers. I bet there is one.'

'Yes, they were always escaping and creeping around in olden days history,' I say. 'We should feel all the walls.'

By the dim lamplight, we start feeling our way across the walls, tap, tap, tapping with the palms of our hands.

Moon Dog gallops to the left back corner of the room and barks.

'Is it over there, boy?' asks Marcus.

'Is this where they bring you in, Moon Dog?' I say.

We run over and start feeling the wall, bit by bit.

'There's a groove here,' says Marcus, 'but my thumb's too big to fit in it.'

'Move out of the way,' I say, and as I push my little thumb into the groove, the whole wall moves backwards. Moon Dog barks, and a passage is before us.

Moon Dog runs through, disappearing into the dark, his bark echoing back at us.

'Quick,' I say, switching on my phone torch, 'before the men come back.'

Marcus has to stoop as the jagged rock roof of the ceiling is so low, which slows him a bit.

'You go ahead,' says Marcus, 'go on, run.'

So I do, with Marcus huffing and puffing behind me.

I am just wondering why the men carried the cages of puppies all the way down the ladder and not through this tunnel, when I step in freezing cold water, getting the answer to my own question.

'Stop, Marcus,' I call behind me. 'Look!'

An underground pool stretches in front of us. Moon Dog is standing on the opposite bank, shaking his coat, a halo of water droplets surrounding him.

The ceiling of the tunnel is high above the pool, so Marcus is able to stand up straight.

'I bet those men sent poor Moon Dog down here by himself, while they use the ladder,' I say.

Marcus pulls off his trainers and socks. Stuffing the socks inside the trainers, he ties the laces together, balances the trainers over his shoulder, and, rolling up his trousers, steps into the water. It comes up to his waist.

'Delilah, I'll give you a piggyback.'

'I'll swim,' I say.

'No,' says Marcus. 'It's stupid for us both to get

wet. You've rescued me by using your smallness. Please, please let me use my tallness to help you.'

As I look into the dark water, I know he's right, and clamber on to his back. I grip my arm round his neck, and hold his trainer laces with a tight fist, so they don't fall in the water. With my other hand, I shine my phone torch in front of us, as Marcus starts to wade to the other side.

Moon Dog barks as we reach the opposite bank. I clamber off Marcus's back and wait as he stuffs his wet feet back into his trainers. No time for socks. We carry on through the tunnel as the ground starts to slope up, and out we come into the night air, on the other side of the hill, between two bushes.

'I'm going to phone Matt the Vet,' says Marcus. 'We must get those dogs out of there. Now!'

'Oh, no,' he says, shaking his phone. 'The battery died. Delilah, you'll have to phone Matt, he'll, know what to do.'

I find Matt's number on my phone and hand it to him. 'Marcus, this is your discovery, you should tell Matt.'

So Marcus makes the call.

22

Marcus

So there we are, waiting back at the top of the hill, between the honeysuckle and the climbing rose. One small person, Delilah, and one big person, me, and between us a ginormous Moon Dog.

Soon we see the parade of vans and cars bumping over the grass towards us. Moon Dog barks, and we jump up and down (I'm partly doing it to keep warm in my wet trousers), shouting, 'WE ARE TREMENDOUS' at the top of our voices, to attract their attention and wave them over.

Matt's Vet On Call car leads the way, followed by an RSPCA van and two police cars.

Matt jumps out of his car and runs over to us

and puts his arms around our shoulders. 'News of this has spread through a network of night phone calls across all the rescue centres in the whole of London. Just look at how many people have got out of their beds to come and help.'

Delilah and I tell the police and an RSPCA inspector called Molly about everything that has happened, and all that we have seen. 'But Nose Ring and Leopard Tattoo might come back at any moment,' I say.

'I hope they do,' says the police officer in charge as she directs two other officers to come forward. 'It will save us having to hunt them down. I am going to station two of my officers up here to keep an eye out for them.' She then circulates a description of Nose Ring and Leopard Tattoo and the van driver on her radio.

Matt directs the vets and people from the rescue centres, sorting them into teams, and telling them what the procedure will be. Marnie waves across to me and Delilah and gives us a thumbs up, then she turns and shouts down the hill, 'Over here!' Lots of people are walking up the hill to join us. They are wearing T-shirts that say *Volunteer* across the front. I spot Miss Raquel and Alf the window cleaner. Word has spread – it seems as if the whole of the dog-loving community are here to help. Miss Raquel shouts over to us.

'I am so proud of you two.'

There is another van bumping over the heath towards us. One I would know anywhere. Out jumps Nana Sparrow, Florence and Dad – MY DAD! – and he runs over and hugs me, like he doesn't want to ever let me go, but we've got work to do and he knows it. Nana has brought some warm clothes for me to change into, and I crouch in the back of her van and I wriggle out of my wet trousers, shirt and bow-tie and into my tracksuit bottoms and big thick jumper.

Ten minutes later, everyone is wearing white or blue PVC boiler suits with hoods, and shoe covers and plastic gloves are handed out. I feel like I'm on a vet TV show. Delilah's is huge on her. Dad laughs, and, taking a big pair of scissors out of his tool bag, he quickly cuts the trousers and arms so they fit her. We all look like strange aliens who have landed on Parliament Hill in the middle of the night.

'I'll look after your fine fellow,' Miss Raquel says, grabbing Moon Dog's collar. 'I am going to stay up here, to keep an eye on people's bags and things.'

'Thanks, Miss,' I say.

'Lead the way, Marcus,' shouts Matt.

I kick the gravel aside, and pull up the manhole cover, and down, down, down, we all go, to dog hell.

And there is a silence, as everyone stands still and looks around them, taking in the horror. Shocked, twisted faces, some blinking back tears and the sound of a police officer openly sobbing. The puppies, each litter huddled together in fear, stare back at us strange plastic-dressed aliens who have come to save them. And as we walk through the cellar, the noise of the dogs' barking rises and rises in a frenzy at the sight of so many people together. Dogs cowering in the back of the cages – feral, petrified; others snarling at the front – fierce, aggressive, unsure.

Then as one, we all set to work.

I take Matt to the back room, squeezing through the gap in the wedged-open door, and show him the mother dogs and newborn pups, staring up at us under the heat lamps. He looks around him, disgust scribbled all over his face.

Evidence is needed, so Molly from the RSPCA takes photo after photo, after photo.

'Please can I help?' says Delilah. 'I want to do my bit.'

'Of course,' says Molly. 'The more evidence the better. We need a photo of each cage with a log of the breed and how many dogs, so that we can keep track of them all.'

Delilah follows Molly, snap, snap, snapping photos of the bedraggled, fearful puppies in their cages with her phone.

Dad starts fixing up temporary lights so that we can all see properly, and as for me, well, I am on the water team, which is a very important job.

Matt said I am useful because I am strong and can lug the big water bottles around. Everyone is doing their bit. I've never seen Florence like this before, it's like she's on a mission, unzipping all the holdalls and organising people to distribute clean water bowls to all the cages. We give fresh water to the thirsty little pups, who lap like they will never stop, and I think of the lovely water going into their little bellies and giving them strength.

I then follow Matt and the team of vets as they examine and assess the puppies and the mother dogs that are being used to breed and breed and breed . . . My heart aches as I hear the vets list all the issues and damage that being in this environment has done to them. Hearing damage from the constant barking, sight problems from being kept in the dark, bad teeth, skin problems, fleas, bone deficiencies, anxiety issues and that's just for starters.

The dogs are loaded into dog carriers, litter by litter, ready to be taken out of here.

With a bark, a very wet Moon Dog comes bounding up to me, puts his paws on my shoulders, nearly knocking me over, and licks my cheek.

'What are you doing down here, Moon Dog?' I say, but I can't be stern, 'cause I am just chuffed to bits he wants to be with me. 'Clever boy, Moon Dog,' I whisper in his ear.

We walk through to the back room, where the police have now forced my prison door fully open. Matt is gently lifting a French bulldog mother into a carrier.

I feel eyes on me. I look up, and Nana Sparrow is watching me and Moon Dog.

And then Delilah is by my side.

'We've done it, Marcus, we've saved over one hundred dogs.' I hold my hand up, and she puts her tiny hand in the palm of mine and whispers, 'You're tremendous, Marcus.'

We form a human chain and start to take the dogs up the ladder. Moon Dog runs back and forth, barking at each dog cage, and I know in my heart he is saying goodbye to his friends of the darkness.

Dogs are supposed to be man's best friend, but I am telling you, this is no way to treat your friends. Those puppy smugglers do not even deserve to breathe the same air as these beautiful dogs.

And we take the puppies out of the dark, up the ladder and into the light, so that they can learn what sky is, what the sun rising is, how it feels to have the breeze rippling through your coat as you run on the heath, or on a beach, with the sea lapping at your paws. To swim through a lake, and run through the trees in a forest, and most importantly, to know what love is and that us human beings can be their friends.

As the last dog carrier is lifted out, I feel my legs want to collapse, but I know I've got to take my Moon Dog round the long way. Except I know he's not mine, no matter how much I pretend. Sadness fills me.

'Come on, boy, come on, Moon Dog.'

'I'm coming with you,' Delilah says. 'We started this together, and we'll finish it together, you, me and Moon Dog. You are not going through the dark alone.'

And we hold hands through the tunnel, and before I can stop Delilah, she says, 'You are too tired to carry me.' She puts her phone in her teeth to keep it dry, and wades into the water. It comes up to her neck. I shove my phone in my mouth and do the same. Moon Dog jumps in, and we hold on to him, and he swims, pulling our tired bones through the freezing underground lake, and we walk through the tunnel, into the rising sun.

Nana Sparrow is standing in the middle of the ruins of Rose Manor Hall, shouting like she's on her fruit and veg stall, and using her sorting-out-potatoes-and-carrots skills to work out which rescue centre is taking which dogs.

Moon Dog starts barking. I look up and see Leopard Tattoo and Nose Ring walk over the brow of the hill. I see them gape at all the people and cars and vans. Then I see them spot the police, and turn and start to run. But their cruelty to dogs fires my feet and I start to run too, Moon Dog running by my side, and as I overtake them and stick my big feet out, Leopard Tattoo goes flying into the path of Nose Ring and they land in a heap on the grass.

The police are right behind me and handcuff them.

Everybody starts to clap. Moon Dog barks as I search for Dad in the crowd and spy him leaning against a tree. I run over to him.

Dad puts his hand on my head.

'Thanks, Dad, for coming out,' I say.

'Of course,' he mutters. 'You were in need of help.'

And then, 'I'm proud of you, son.'

And we just smile at each other like we will never stop.

Matt and Delilah come sprinting up to me.

'Marcus,' says Matt, 'I am going to take Moon Dog back with me. I need to check him over, and he is going to have to go into quarantine for parvo as he has been near dogs with the virus.' Matt squeezes my arm. 'I will look after him, Marcus. It's just a precaution.'

I nod and bite my lip hard. I fling myself down on my knees, hugging my Moon Dog, only I know he's not mine, no matter how much I wish it. Delilah puts her arm around my waist as Moon Dog is loaded into the car, and I look into my dog friend's eyes as he is driven away, until he is nothing but a black dot.

23

Marcus

Nana has got me hoovering and dusting and polishing. Though not her figurines – she doesn't trust me with those, ever since that china lady's head came off.

'We must make the house spick and span,' she says. 'We have a visitor.'

Dad's gone back to his bed with the leg made of books. Even though he told me he was proud of me. It doesn't seem like his son getting held prisoner by dog smugglers underground then helping arrest dog smugglers in an all-night dog-rescue operation will get him out of that bed for good. I GIVE UP.

The doorbell rings, and when I run to open it, Delilah and Florence are standing there.

'Delilah, I didn't know you were coming round,' I say.

'I don't have to tell you everything, do I?' She pushes past me.

'Come in, come in,' says Nana, 'make yourselves at home.'

We sit at the table and have turnip soup, which is all right, as it goes. It's much nicer than the turnip cake we had for tea yesterday.

Delilah seems a bit jiggly; she can't sit still.

The doorbell rings again.

'Go and answer it please, Marcus,' says Nana.

So I do as I'm told. Matt the Vet is walking away from the door towards his car that is parked at the end of our path, and I look down to see Moon Dog staring back up at me. He gives me his paw, and there is a label attached to his collar. It says, **I belong to Marcus Sparrow**.

I fall on my knees.

Finally, Moon Dog is mine! I hug my beautiful Moon Dog.

Then everything begins to move in slow motion as he leaps over me and runs up the stairs. We all follow him up and into Dad's bedroom, where he jumps on the bed, right on top of Dad. There is a creak, and the bed with the leg made of books collapses. There's a heap of ginormous dog with Dad's arms and legs sticking out either side of him, waving around like octopus tentacles, and everyone gasps at the same time, like you see in cartoons. Then there is this silence as we watch and wait, followed by a snort from Dad that becomes a chuckle, that becomes a laugh, then a guffaw, and soon we are all laughing too. My dad can't go back to bed now. He's got no bed to go back to.

Moon Dog climbs off Dad, lying next to him on the mattress on the floor, surrounded by books.

'Isn't this the same dog who was with you at the night rescue?'

'Meet Moon Dog,' I say.

'He's come to live with us,' says Nana Sparrow.

'For ever, Nana?' I say.

'For ever, Marcus,' says Nana. 'You deserve this. We've got to go down to the rescue home and sign the adoption papers this afternoon.'

I can't stop grinning. I HAVE A DOG!

Dad ruffles Moon Dog's fur.

'Who's a beautiful big teddy bear of a dog then?' he says, hugging Moon Dog. 'Who's a great big beautiful dog?' And then they're rolling around together, my Moon Dog and my dad, surrounded by broken bed legs and books.

'Can I take your Moon Dog for a walk, son, while you're signing the papers?'

'Yes, Dad, but take care of him, please.' And I take my dog lead out of my pocket and hand it to him. I know that my dad has a long road to recovery from his sadness but maybe taking Moon Dog for a walk will be a start.

'I promise, Marcus.'

'I know, Dad.'

We go to the Beckham Animal Rescue Centre in Nana's van. The receptionist lets us through to the back, and we walk past a row of dogs in kennels. Many from our rescue. All looking happy now, waiting for their forever homes.

'We should call your dog Spud, really, because I am paying for him out of the potato money,' says Nana.

'No, he's Moon Dog.'

'I like the name Spud,' says Florence.

'So do I like Spud,' calls out Delilah, who is kneeling down in front of one of the kennels.

There is a tiny yapping, and a little chihuahua with three legs and one eye runs forward, wagging his tail.

'Spud, Spud, do you like that name?' says Delilah, to the little dog.

'Yap, yap,' barks the chihuahua.

Delilah jumps up. 'Mum,' she whispers, 'please, Mum, he's the one.'

Florence crouches down next to Delilah, and holds her hand out. The little dog sniffs it.

'OK then, let's talk to them in the office.'

Marnie is in the office when we all troop in.

'Hello, Marcus and Delilah,' she says, smiling the biggest of smiles. 'You are our rescue dog heroes! Ten of the puppies we rescued that night already have their forever homes thanks to you.'

'Please,' says Delilah, 'tell me about that little three-legged chihuahua?'

'Oh, Frank! He's such a friendly little fellow. He was found abandoned in a car park. Can you believe it? Are you interested in adopting him?'

Delilah nods, hopping from one foot to the other. 'I'd call him Spud,' she says.

'I know about your little dachshund,' says Marnie. 'The RSPCA will need to give clearance, because the parvo contaminated your living space. I am afraid you will need to wait a while, until they know your home's safe. I'm sorry but it could take a year.'

Delilah crumples on to a chair.

'You also need time to grieve for Chip,' says Florence.

I see a sign on the wall that says *Fosterers Needed* and suddenly I have an idea to help my friend.

'Would we be allowed to foster him at our house until Delilah's flat is safe?' I ask.

Nana Sparrow smiles. 'Sounds like a solution.'

'Oh, please, please, please,' says Delilah.

'We'll need to check that Moon Dog and Frank – sorry, Spud – get on,' says Marnie.

'Oh, Moon Dog gets on with everyone,' I say.

We munch chocolate digestives, and drink tea, and listen, as Marnie talks about responsible dog ownership.

Then comes the big moment.

Nana signs Moon Dog's adoption papers and I sign **Marcus Sparrow** underneath. Moon Dog is officially my very own dog.

24

Delilah

Marcus and I are outside the law court. I have Spud on a lead, and Marcus has Moon Dog. They are our rescue dogs and we are proud.

Marcus and I are part of a crowd of people wearing *#AdoptDontShop* T-shirts, a slogan to encourage people to go to rescue centres to get a dog.

Nana Sparrow and Mum are with us, wearing their T-shirts too. Mum is waving an ADOPT DON'T SHOP placard high in the air. Since that overnight rescue, Mum has stopped texting me every few minutes and constantly wringing her hands. She has purpose in her day now. She has become a puppy rights activist, talking about Chip to newspapers, TV, radio, and anyone else who will listen to her, raising awareness about the evils of puppy farming.

A prison van drives up to the pavement where we have gathered. Leopard Tattoo and Nose Ring are inside. Today they are being sentenced by the judge for puppy smuggling and cruelty to animals. The crowd starts to chant, 'Adopt, don't shop. Adopt, don't shop. Adopt, don't shop.'

And as the chant gets louder, Marcus and I slip away for our promised walk in memory of Chip, a brave little puppy who never stood a chance, but whose life meant so much.

We scatter red and blue petals, then we sing our song.

'We are le le le lead walking . . .'

But we change the second line to:

'We've both got dogs
Lead walking through the park and the bog
We are lead walking . . .'

My little Spud manages so brilliantly with his three legs and one eye. If he can be brave, then so can I be brave. We give each other courage. It's me and Spud from now on. There isn't a day that goes by when I don't miss my dad, the man who liked sunshine and old records, books to make you grow and trips to exciting places. I loved him so very much, but I know he would want me to be happy and with Spud by my side, I can be.

I glance sideways at Marcus, looking so proud with his Moon Dog. The big dog with the big boy.

'Swap,' I say, 'you walk Spud, and I will walk Moon Dog.'

'Oh, all right then,' he says, giving me Moon Dog's lead, and people stare at me, the tiny girl with the ginormous Newfoundland, and Marcus the ginormous boy with the tiny chihuahua, as we walk along, singing our song.

We walk up the hill to our place, Rose Manor Hall. Between the rose and the honeysuckle, we scatter the rest of the petals for Chip, and all the dogs that were kept down there in the dark, and all the dogs that have ever suffered at the hands of cruel people.

Marcus's phone rings and he answers it.

He goes red in the face, and his eyes shine.

'Yes . . . Yes . . . that's brilliant. Thank you so much . . . Can I tell Delilah? She's right next to me. We are walking our dogs . . . Thank you . . . Goodbye.'

'What, what, Marcus?' I say, hopping from one foot to the other.

'Delilah, there is this award ceremony called The Animal and People of Courage Awards and guess what? We've won **Young Dog Rescuers of the Year**. You and me and Moon Dog! They are going to give him a special rosette. We are going up to Mansion House, with everyone who was there that night, and the Mayor of London is going to give us the award in a big ceremony, with lots of cake and everything.'

Tears of joy splash down my cheeks. This award will honour Chip's life. I never want other children to go through what me and Chip went through, and with Spud and Moon Dog by our side, me and Marcus can spread the word, because we are the Young Dog Rescuers of the Year.

Marcus holds his hand out and I fit my tiny hand in his palm, and together we shout, 'WE ARE TREMENDOUS.'

THE STORY BEHIND MOON DOG

Saying 'Goodbye, I love you' to Crayon, my little kitten, who I had only had for a day, was one of the hardest things I have ever had to do. It was four o'clock in the morning and I was at the vet's, still in my pyjamas with my coat pulled over the top, completely heartbroken. The nurse was waiting in the street for my taxi and ushered me in as I clutched a box with my tiny kitten curled up on a blanket fighting for life. Crayon lost the battle but had fought so very hard. Danny Parry the vet and the nurses at Village Vets were oh-so kind. But from that moment my life was changed.

You see, I had bought little Crayon from a pet store (thankfully now no longer trading). I had been so worried as the tiny kitten looked alone and fretful in a cage and I wanted to give her a loving home. But when I went to tell them that my kitten had died of an E. coli infection, they didn't care. Instead, they tried to give me two older kittens that they couldn't sell. To them, animals were just a money-making commodity, not living breathing souls.

I donated all of Crayon's food and never-played-with toys to North London Cats Protection. My mum came round to my flat to help me pack up all of my kitten stuff and we took it round to the charity. And so began my education on rescue animals. When they looked at Crayon's photograph they said they could tell my kitten was too young to be away from the mother cat. They also told me that they felt I would make a good fosterer for Cats Protection. This I did, fostering, then adopting a blind ginger cat with wobbly legs called Griffid, and then later Larry, a retired one-eyed alley cat with no teeth and cauliflower ears who I adopted from The Celia Hammond Animal Trust, for the last two years of his life. Having rescue animals in my life was the most rewarding thing I had ever done.

But the pain and anger at Crayon's short life never left me and I couldn't bear to think of other people, especially children, going through the pain that I had been through of losing a new puppy or kitten. I started to educate myself on the terrible puppy farm trade. Puppies bred in terrible conditions on a mass scale purely for profit, often smuggled all crammed together in the back of a van from Eastern Europe. I also learned about the puppy farms in Ireland and Wales, many of these actually licensed, and the scale of these operations is beyond belief. This is a trade that deals in sick and dying puppies. I knew that I had to write a book about it.

I then went on to watch some truly excellent, though harrowing, documentaries.

Grace Victory's brilliant *The Cost of Cute: The Dark Side of the Puppy Trade* was the starting point of inspiration for me. I then went on to watch Matt Allwright's *Rogue Traders* episode on puppy farming, Samantha Poling's *Panorama: Britain's Puppy Dealers Exposed* as well as her documentary, *The Dog Factory*, on BBC Scotland. While writing this book I watched an episode of *Animal Rescue Live* where Noel Fitzpatrick locked himself in a cage and was driven for miles, in the back of a van, for six hours to replicate the long journey that many of these puppies make when smuggled into the country. This had such a profound effect on me and geared me on to meet my deadline!

It was the UNILAD documentary, *The Dark Side of Britain: Puppy Farms*, that also helped lay the foundation for my writing *Moon Dog*.

Enter *#LucysLaw* and the most amazing animal campaigners into my life. Lucy's Law, passed through Parliament in spring 2020, requires puppies and kittens to be born and raised in a safe environment with their mothers and sold from the place they were born in.

Firstly, I would like to pay tribute to Lucy herself, the brave and beautiful Cavalier King Charles spaniel whose story sparked off the campaign. Her life started off in tragedy as a puppy farm dog kept in a cage and used to breed from but ended her years being loved and cherished by Lisa Garner, who campaigned tirelessly for Lucy's Law. I salute you and all the team who campaigned; in particular I would like to mention:

Eileen Jones (Friends of the Animals Wales) – Eileen, I have watched with awe from afar all you do to rescue puppy farm dogs.

Peter Egan – you must be applauded for everything you do to campaign for animal rights.

Linda Goodman (CARIAD), thank you so, so much for taking the time to talk to me; your help was invaluable in writing *Moon Dog*. All the broken dogs that you heal, so that they can become a whole dog again, is truly incredible. I respect you so much.

And last but not least, Marc Abraham (Pup Aid) or 'Marc the Vet' as he is known. It was an absolute privilege to listen to you talk about your campaign with such passion and I am so proud to wear the Lucy's Law rosette you presented me with for my author events and interviews to raise awareness.

I would like to give thanks to Luke Balsam from Luke's Dog School for putting me in touch with the above campaigners and for your support and to also thank Susie McKenna who first told me about parvovirus, which sowed the very first seed of *Moon Dog*.

This book would not have been written without the support and knowledge of vet Duncan D'Arcy-Howard from the RVC. Duncan: Larry, my rescue cat, was so privileged to have you as his vet to see him through the last stages of his life, and I give my thanks beyond measure for your continued kindness, support, knowledge and patience with my endless questions about parvovirus.

Thank you to Superintendent Simon Osborne from the RSPCA for your guidance.

It was so special to meet Bob the Newfoundland and Dawn Richardson, his human, at the Discover Dogs exhibition. Dawn, thank you for answering all my questions about Newfs and their drooling and their general loveliness!

Katrina Baranyi, thank you for your guidance with Delilah's hair and for keeping my own unruly mop tamed so beautifully so I could see to write my book!

And talking of sight, thank you Mr Saurabh Jain for operating on my eyes and enabling me to see the words.

Hilary McKay, thank you for sharing with me your wondrous nature knowledge.

Naomi Greenwood, my truly amazing editor at Hodder Children's Books, for your skill in helping *Moon Dog* flourish, and Jodie Hodges, my agent, for encouraging my original idea to grow. Michelle Brackenborough for your amazing cover design and to my publicists, Dom Kingston and Becci Mansell, for your warmth, energy and support.

Christopher Ryan, for taking the photograph of me with Abi the Staffie – Ambassador for charity All Dogs Matter. Abi, thank you for posing for the camera so beautifully!

Friends and family and supporters: Sharon D. Clarke MBE, Marcia Mantack, Tracey Smith, Sally Randles, Doctor Emily Randles, Semsem Kuherhi, Paul Neaum, Steve Antony, Kristina Stephenson, Tameka Empson, Jenny Elson, Christopher William Hill, Patrice Lawrence, Curtis Ashton, Lou Kuenzler, Annie Everall OBE, Clare Calder and also my writing group – huge thank you to you all for cheering me on to the finishing line.

And finally I would like to pay tribute to Ira Moss and her amazing team at charity All Dogs Matter. It is my honour and privilege to witness the utterly amazing work you do rehoming abandoned and unwanted dogs from the UK and overseas. You transform lives daily and I am so proud to know you.

Jane Elson

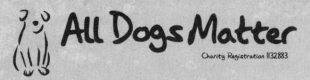

All Dogs Matter

Charity Registration 1132883

If you are considering adopting a dog and live in London and the surrounding areas, please consider adopting from All Dogs Matter.

All Dogs Matter is a dog rescue and rehoming charity working in and around London to transform the lives of unwanted and abandoned dogs. We also rehome dogs in need from overseas.

In 2019 All Dogs Matter rescued and rehomed over 370 dogs with new owners. We also found forever homes for 27 unwanted and abandoned dogs from China, Italy and Egypt.

All Dogs Matter.co.uk

@AllDogsMatter

All Dogs Matter

Abi was just a tiny puppy when she was found in a cardboard box. She now plays an important role as Ambassador for All Dogs Matter.

Photograph by Christopher Ryan

JANE ELSON

After performing as an actress and comedy improviser, Jane fell into writing stories and plays. Her books have won many awards, including Peters Book of the Year two years running. Her debut novel, *A Room Full of Chocolate* was longlisted for the Branford Boase Award and Jane has twice been nominated for the Carnegie Medal.

In *Moon Dog*, Jane is thrilled to return to the world of the Beckham Estate, also featured in multi-award winning *How to Fly With Broken Wings* and *Will you Catch Me?*.

Jane is loud and proud about her dyslexia and when not writing likes to mentor neurodiverse young people, promoting the gift of alternative thinking. She was honoured to be named as one of the top 50 Influential Neurodivergent Women by Women Beyond The Box.

Jane is an advocate for Nacoa and All Dogs Matter, charities close to her heart, and has enjoyed meeting lots of dogs during her research for *Moon Dog*, including Bob the Newfoundland and Abi the Staffie, pictured above with Jane.

www.aroomfullofwords.com

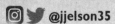 @jjelson35

ALSO AVAILABLE

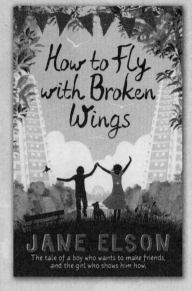

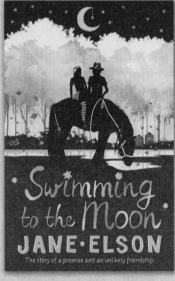